To the Promised Land is the third installment of philosopher-novelist Michael Boylan's ingenious four volume exploration of some of life's great quandaries. Each of the De Anima Novels views fundamental challenges through the lens of the world's great religious perspectives, letting the reader slip into the characters' lives as they grapple with such issues as sudden wealth, racial identity, politics, and fate. *To the Promised Land* gives us powerful individuals wrestling with the conflict between responsibility to ourselves and others, as their tales are paired with insights from the Jewish idea of forgiveness.

Set against the backdrop of the disappearance of guilt-ridden-corporate-attorney-turned-activist Moses Levi, the spine of the story is the attempt of Peter Simon, Levi's former college roommate, to get out from under the thumb of the FBI, who suspect him of Moses' murder. Using a combination of flashbacks, diaries, and eavesdropping on the private musings of various characters, Boylan constructs a rich chronicle that spans more than three decades. The joy and anguish of the pair in college. A stolen love. Levi's longing to be forgiven for winning a Love Canal-like case for his corporate client. Simon's feeling that he's being sandbagged into completing Levi's work. Ego. Classic D.C. organizational intrigue. The challenges of a new relationship. Relief and resolution. And the occasional philosophical excursus. Boylan masterfully weaves the strands into a quilt whose different textures and hues teach us that life, like a good novel, requires complexity to be challenging, meaningful and satisfying.

TO THE PROMISED LAND
A Novel of Freedom and Redemption

Michael Boylan

PWI Books
Bethesda, MD

Cover Design by Greg Simanson
Edited by Joanna Jensen
Proofread by Samantha March
Majanka Verstraete, Book Manager

This is a work of fiction. Names, characters, places, brands, media, and incidents are either the product of the author's imagination or are used fictitiously. Any resemblance to similarly named places or to persons living or deceased is unintentional.

ISBN 13: 978-0692-729113 (PWI)
ISB N 10: 069-2729119
Library of Congress Control Number: 2015909016

THE DE ANIMA NOVELS

Rainbow Curve

The Extinction of Desire

To the Promised Land

Maya

FOREWORD

Wanda Teays

TO THE PROMISED LAND--*A Novel of Freedom and Redemption* is a welcome addition to literary philosophy. Like his Existential predecessors Jean Paul Sartre and Albert Camus, Simone de Beauvoir and Iris Murdoch, Michael Boylan has found an effective way of bringing ideas to life. His is an inquiry into the stickiness of being-in-the-world—when persons whose egos outstrip their talents struggle to put their lives in order, but, lacking a sense of direction, see no clear path to do so.

The novel presents us with a cast of characters confronting a set of ethical issues. Decisions have to be made. Consequences follow. Not all are without regret. Not all are praiseworthy. So it is that moral reflection—if not action—is required. More decisions and yet more consequences ensue. We follow at a safe distance, able to watch and learn as the story unfolds.

Boylan builds on his earlier novels *The Extinction of Desire* and *Rainbow Curve*, by shining a light on the various ethical challenges that we confront. Thanks to his fictional springboard, we see how unwarranted assumptions and moral failings can wreak havoc. He shows us that *this* choice can lead to *that* set of consequences. How we handle them lays the groundwork for the moral results. Sizing ourselves up in a moment of reflection may give us some peace of mind, allowing us to infer that a life of integrity, of authenticity, is within our grasp. That's on a good day—not all self-inventories lead to high scores. When we glance backward and tally up the virtues and subtract the moral weight of vices, the result may give us pause.

When our shortcomings outweigh our strengths and all hope for becoming a moral exemplar is lost, ethical assessment is in order. We must then take stock of where we've been and where in the world we're headed. This is the situation facing the two protagonists of *To the Promised Land*. Both find themselves adrift with no helping hand coming to their rescue.

In *A Just Society*, Boylan examines the four cardinal virtues— courage, justice, wisdom, and self-control. He considers these virtues instrumental in constructing a personal worldview. Together they lay the foundation of moral development. Without courage, we are either weak or reckless. Without justice, we lose our sense of fair play, of balance. Without wisdom, we cannot grasp the lessons of the past or apply them to the present. And without self-control, we are prone to excess or losing perspective. However, with these four moral pillars in place we can more easily find our way, guided by a sense of direction.

To the Promised Land presents us with protagonists who fall short on the scale of these four virtues. Both characters are less than admirable. Both are flawed and slow to acknowledge their limitations. Their stories and ethical dilemmas demonstrate how personal worldviews collide. Decisions made in haste or on shaky ground can haunt us years later. That is when we realize that some things can't be undone, that no amount of money or words of contrition can heal all wounds. And so we find ourselves in moral sludge unable to extricate ourselves. Boylan takes us into this moral territory and invites us to see how the issues raised here in this novel are not so different from those each of us face in our own lives.

This is shown in the novel with respect to forgiveness. One of the moral hurdles is: "Are some acts unforgivable acts?" Are there decisions and actions that do not merit forgiveness? And what of those acts that may qualify for forgiveness but it is not forthcoming? What then?

There are two levels that Boylan examines. One is that of the individual, where we look at one person's pain and sense of betrayal. Can they forgive those who caused this suffering? It wasn't deserved, bonds of trust were broken, dreams were turned to dust. What hope is there to let that all go, pretend it didn't matter any more? Can we really forgive? Can we? He raises this in the novel and sets out the dilemma in stark terms:

Powerful stuff. Forgiveness is an intimate human interaction between two individuals. There are two parties: the person who has offended (A) and the person who has been injured (B). A cannot be forgiven unless he solicits forgiveness from B and B agrees to forgive him. It is within B's discretion to forgive or not to forgive.

It doesn't end there: "*This whole model works fine on the level of a two-party interaction,*" Boylan says through his character. "*But what happens when there is 1502 times ten—or more?*"

This question leads us to the second level, where we encounter forgiveness on a grand scale. When entire groups of people are harmed due to malevolence or negligence, the question of forgiveness is more problematic. If *you* harm *us* where we can't come together and deliberate, how can forgiveness be within reach? How can the few speak for the many?

I cannot be forgiven of my sin against other people (from the human point of view) unless those very people who I have injured forgive me. Fifteen hundred and two people died. Imagine how many people were affected—at least five to ten times that amount. How can I personally confront fifteen thousand people?

And furthermore, "*What recourse is there for crimes against Humanity?. . . I have been an accessory to a crime against Humanity.*"

Boylan's character, Moses Levi, is tied in knots, seeking the path to forgiveness, knowing the road ahead is filled with obstacles and there's simply no easy route that can be taken. He asks—and we readers are called to answer:

"*What is there for me to do in these circumstances?*"

The novel gives us a lot to think about in trying to answer that question.

WORKS CITED

Boylan, Michael, *A Just Society*, (Lanham, MD and Oxford: Rowman & Littlefield, 2004)—non-fiction, philosophy.

CHAPTER ONE

Peter Simon

July 5, 2000

NOBODY WAS MORE SURPRISED than I was when Moses vanished. It was so sudden. One minute he had been leading his followers and the next—gone! As you probably read in the newspapers, twenty-four hours after his disappearance I was brought in for questioning by the FBI. The things they did to me only reinforce all my prejudices against the police.

Hoover was his name. Yeah, that's right. Can you believe it? Hoover. Henry Hoover. Federal Bureau of Investigation. Young Nazi with a gun.

"Isn't it true that Moses Levi has been trying to get you to help him with some program he's working on?" Hoover was ten years younger than I and so athletically fit that I wanted to shoot him. Not an ounce of fat on his body. Not an ounce of compassion either.

"No," I replied.

Hoover grabbed my shoulders with hands of steel. They were a vice.

"No!" I repeated, wishing that these proceedings were video recorded instead of merely taped.

"How can you say that?" Hoover's eyebrows raised and his mouth scrunched up into a small circle. "We have documents that—"

"You have documents. The world has television footage. So what?"

"What do you mean, 'so what'?" The vice turned another notch. Where was my attorney? The college said he'd be over in a flash, but there was also a hint of 'moral turpitude.' Moral turpitude, baby. The only way they can kick you out of a tenured spot in your college.

What did it matter if I were innocent? A hint of stain. Bad publicity. Downnnnnn the t u b e s.

Splat. Gone. So long. Thanks for twenty years of servitude at low pay to bring culture to upper middle class brats who couldn't care less. So long.

"Aah," I grunted.

The vice got tighter. I thought I heard a tendon or something start to snap.

"You asked the wrong question."

This did the trick. Hoover decided to stop sucking up my skeletal anatomy and bounced backward as if he had never heard of a wrong question. I think there are probably many things this Neanderthal has never heard of. But that was not my job. Or was it? (A philosophy professor cannot turn it on and turn it off.)

"What?"

"The game. The question. You ask. I answer."

"You asshole," said Hoover as he came after me again.

"What you need to know," I began, but stopped because of the pain as he pulled back my right arm (the one that I hurt on the swim team in high school). "Holy shit!" I screamed.

Hoover stepped back again.

"Your question should be if Moses asked me if I were interested in bringing my clients, who are among the shining stars in the Fairfax County business community—especially the law firm of Cohen, Potts, and Sani—-to help his Fair Opportunity Program. That is the question you need to ask. Not whether he asked me to actually help him."

"What?" Hoover was out of his element.

"The difference is this- case one: Moses asks me to help him in his new program; or case two: Moses inquires about my *interest* in helping him in his new program."

Hoover's silence told me he didn't understand. This braced me a bit. So I ventured, "The first case indicates that he really wanted me to *do* something. The second is rather different. Here he asks me about *potential* interest—no sense of urgency or implied consent." I leaned forward, gesturing with my hands. "Now do you see the difference?"

Hoover turned around and walked toward the wall. Then he reached into the pocket of his "dry clean only" gray pants and pulled out a handkerchief. The FBI man tried to wipe his forehead that was beginning to perspire.

Then Hoover pivoted and said (a bit more loudly), "Can you get off your high and mighty university language and just answer the question?"

It occurred to me at that moment that there were probably few subjects that agent Hoover and I could discuss in a free and dispassionate manner.

*   *   *

They let me go home.

This was a good thing. I wanted to go home to see whether Monique had returned yet. She said she was going out with some friends for the Fourth, I understand that, but she promised that she'd be back today. I live in a pre-World War II home in North Arlington. It's not far from Notre Dame-Loyola where I teach. I turn past the Safeway and then a right and down a couple blocks to a quiet, secluded old house that we remodeled five years ago. It's full of space and quiet in a neighborhood full of nice people.

When I pulled in (around seven o'clock) Monique was not there. This was unusual. Monique worked part-time at George Washington University (GW—for short), and was generally very regular in her hours. This regularity in habits was what first attracted her to me. I knew that I could never live with someone with an odd time schedule.

I sat down in my gray leather chair, poured myself a double whiskey and turned on the news. Sometimes I wonder why they call it the 'news.' What is really 'new' about it? "People die in a war/famine/natural disaster." "There is the most scandalous thing happening in government!" "Rain predicted for the weekend."

The names in this story have been changed to protect our sense of sanity.

I turned to my right and picked up a pile of student papers. I was supposed to have turned these things back two weeks ago. But things have been tough. I had to take Monique down to Hilton Head for a conference. And then there was all the fuss that Moses made. Smoke and mirrors. Pressure to make me help him. Help him. Ha!

Then the doorbell rang. I swallowed my drink and put on my game face. No. It wasn't Monique (I don't know why I even thought it would be her when she lived here and never rang the doorbell). No, it was the Federal Express person who handed me a second day envelope that certainly contained more than a letter. I was totally clueless. I went back to my chair and deposited the package, poured myself a triple and opened the packet.

It was from Moses.

To Peter,

This is my journal. I know that you will know what to do with it.

Moses

Just like Moses. Puts you on the spot. I opened the journal and began to read:

THE JOURNAL OF MOSES LEVI:
JUNE 6, 1987

I guess I won. I did what I had to do. What all lawyers are supposed to do: represent your client and give him the best defense you can. But what if your client hurt other people and you helped him get off? Aren't you then a part of the process that has hurt others? Isn't this wrong? Am I not wrong? There are thousands of people who were hurt by my client. Many will die. Many will be disabled. If you count the extended families the count is multiplied by five or six. What have I done? What have I done?

CHAPTER TWO

Peter Simon

July 5, 2000

MOSES' JOURNAL SURPRISED ME as much as Henry Hoover taking me down to headquarters. I never even knew that Moses kept a journal. And why (even if he had) did he send it to me? You see, Moses Levi has been out of my life for almost twenty years. I really had no interest in keeping up with him—even though we *had* been college roommates for two years. No, I would have been just fine if Moses Levi had never called me a few months ago about his big project. *Time Magazine* and *Newsweek* both put him on their covers and wrote extensive stories on his Humanity Hospital Case that he has parlayed into a national debate on Affirmative Action (that he depicts as the Fair Opportunity Initiative).

Really there is so little hard, tough philosophical debate in his writing it is pathetic. After all, he did do an undergraduate major in philosophy at Pembroke and a year of graduate study in philosophy at the University of Chicago before transferring to the law school.

Curiosity made me want to read his journal further.

THE JOURNAL OF MOSES LEVI:
JUNE 7, 1987

I haven't slept much since the verdict. I think that I will have to proceed backwards and sort things out for myself or else I will go mad. Everything that I pretended to believe in is now being called into question. Waste Disposal Systems, Inc. A huge client. What more could I have wished for at this point in my career? A way to make a big splash. An almost impossible case so that any progress that I made would be seen as a success.

The facts: 1. Waste Disposal Systems, Inc. was formed in 1965 to be a contractor to handle industry's waste products. These included toxic and non-toxic substances. 2. Waste Disposal Systems, Inc. aggressively sought clients who had toxic waste problems (since they perceived that they might have a problem in light of the growing environmental movement and would pay the most). 3. Waste Disposal Systems, Inc. acquired a lucrative contract with Wod Chemical (one of the largest chemical companies in the world). 4. Waste Disposal Systems, Inc. set up three disposal sites for Wod: one in upstate New York, one in South Carolina, and one in Utah.

None of the sites were contrary to U.S. Government regulations. Each involved the creation of a large pit (generally eight stories deep). Each pit was lined with a layer of clay that was then hardened with a chemical substance so that (it was thought) an impenetrable seal was formed.

But the clay and the seal proved to be porous.

THE JOURNAL OF MOSES LEVI: JUNE 8, 1987

Why did I go into law? In the beginning it was the idealism. No, that isn't so. In the beginning it was because I saw that there were not enough jobs in philosophy and because I greatly enjoyed Edward Levi's course on Jurisprudence in Society. The man was a master. He had the theoretical knowledge and he also had the practical experience as the former president of the University of Chicago and as the Attorney General of the United States.

Levi (you can't fault a man for having an excellent name) was a little more conservative than I, but at that time of my life it didn't matter. The man was a genius. That was what turned me to law.

THE JOURNAL OF MOSES LEVI: JUNE 9, 1987

I feel as if I am living in a black hole. Everything is upside down. You realize what I have allowed myself to become? I have always despised nominalism. Various philosophers have tried to "solve" a problem with merely a thin semantic solution. Yet here am I, an advocate of a company charged with a very serious offense and I based my case on just that. Waste Disposal perhaps began in good faith. They met the existing government regulations exactly. Doesn't this mean that they were a model corporate citizen? They kept to the letter of the law?

But even as they were executing their very lucrative business deal the regulative climate was changing. The environmental movement was making converts of various members of Congress who were holding hearings on this and other issues.

It was clear to anyone who read the record that the laws were going to change. The stages might take a decade or so to complete, but this entire strategy (which was really rather inexpensive) would be deemed unacceptable. Waste Disposal knew this. Wod and their other clients knew this, too. That is why they wanted someone else to take on the liability of these toxic chemicals. Wod knew there was a problem so they decided to unload it upon Waste Disposal.

The facts: The clay seals did not hold. The chemical waste broke through the seal and into the surrounding land at all angles. In New York State the surrounding area was heavily populated. The toxic chemicals invaded the ground water and formed toxic "channels" that under houses such that fumes penetrated the very foundations of houses as they moved upward. This meant that families, especially those living at home – children and their mothers – were most at risk.

The net effect in New York State was that twenty-four hundred and forty-nine people in the affected area developed cancer — 100 times the amount that would have been statistically expected from such a sample space.

Waste Disposal killed these people. I successfully defended Waste Disposal. Quod Erat Demonstratum, I am an accessory to murder.

I didn't formulate any clear thoughts on the bit of the journal I read for a couple of days. Monique called and told me she had to visit her mother in New Jersey. This seemed odd since in the three years that we have lived together, Monique has never visited her mother. I'm not sure she has even mentioned her mother. The karma seemed very bad with Monique. She was probably seeing someone else and trying to determine whether Number Two's added excitement is worth his not having a steady income. I mean, I pull in 75K from my teaching, but then I score another 125K from my consulting work. You cannot believe how lucrative consulting work is around the Washington, DC area!

Well, in my mind, I guess I have to bid Monique bye-bye. Though I really liked her a lot. In so many ways I wish she'd stay around a little longer. I could really relax with her. No demands—nothing like Julia. Julia turned me off completely from the idea of marriage. She is the dialectical opposite of Monique. (I'm a Hegelian scholar, you know, so that's meant to be a little joke. Perhaps a very little joke.)

At any rate, we will see whether Monique's libido prefers a sexual superman over a man who can put her up at the Ritz.

Getting back to the journal. You must know that university professors, like me, digress. We are given no classes in education during graduate school and the only thing we know about teaching (now that pipe smoking is verboten) is to enter into long digressions that never lead anywhere. It's a pedagogical device designed to allow the student to finish it for himself.

Such an answer is both true and bullshit. It is bullshit if the professor is not sincere in his digressions. But if he is, then it is the best sort of teaching that exists. The same holds true in philosophical literature. Ultimately, it is not only about the truth of the argument that is presented. It is also about the vision of *what is* that the philosopher presents. In this way the philosopher becomes a storyteller. And it is the storyteller who is the person who holds communities together.

Concerning the June 7th entry. Moses is really reacting to the disparity between being a person who follows the letter of the law and one who follows some broader, natural law scheme. This leads to some traditional problems. On the one hand, when we rely upon the written law as our sole guide to action, then we are often presented with a situation in which the written law is confronted with a situation that the framers did not envision. If the written law is all there is (legal positivism), then much injustice can occur. This is because there may be many gaps between accepted precedents. These gaps are fulfilled only by judicial discretion.

Natural law theorists, on the other hand, cite eternal laws (generally associated with God) that supersede human law. When human law is inadequate, then natural law steps in. Because these natural laws are rather more abstract than legal precedents, it is never the case that one might fall between precedents in which there is no compelling imperative. However, sometimes there is a dispute about what controlling abstract principle covers the particular case at hand. But this is a smaller problem.

Natural law is the perfect answer to an age-old question.

Unfortunately, as you know, philosophers are among the meanest creatures on the planet. They have not flocked over to my side. This is because they are driven by petty jealousies and turf battles. However, my corporate clients appreciate the way that I am able to navigate about seemingly intractable difficulties.

What happened to Moses is that he acted purely as an advocate of another, his client. This is what the legal profession is often based upon. But there is an inherent contradiction in such a stance. Each person must be responsible for upholding the *Sittlichkeit*. In this case there are a number of established principles of personal integrity that would be violated in simply becoming the servant of one's client. (One is reminded of the master-slave dialectic in the *Phenomenology of Spirit.*)

When Moses allowed himself merely to be the instrument of his client, then he became the slave. The slave achieves his identity through the reflection of the master. The master, in this case, was a multi-national company that was intent on acting profitably just at the line of the letter of (but not the spirit of) the law. This is not unusual behavior for many successful businesses. They feel that if their marginal return of money to investors (who own the company) increases as one gets closer to the actual legal line and many even ride a few ticks *over* the line along with a good alibi. The potential return of money on such positioning is significant. However, I advise my clients that the added profit isn't worth it.

"But don't you owe your stockholders the highest possible return on their money? Isn't that what fiduciary responsibility is all about?"

"No," I say. "The *Sittlichkeit* of Occidental Culture is such that you will sacrifice too much by taking that gambit. The stockholders deserve a fair return but not the highest possible return. What I mean by this is a return that is within pale of decent behavior. If maximizing money were the only imperative, then we'd be importing heroin or selling illegal weapons to rogue nations."

Moses seems to have missed this point. He got caught up in the Legal Code of Ethics that seems to absolve lawyers of doing anything wrong. It is as if they are not real people at all but merely machines that do the bidding of their masters.

The fallacy of this argument is demonstrated by our societal abhorrence of the so-called excuse that some Nazis gave, "I was only following orders!" As if we could strip away personal responsibility in such a way. I read further in Moses' journal.

THE JOURNAL OF MOSES LEVI: JUNE 14, 1987

Facts: 1. Waste Disposal did not break the law when it acted as it did. 2. If one obeys the law, then he should not be prosecuted by the law. 3. Both Waste Disposal and Wod knew the law was woefully inadequate and was in the process of being changed. 4. Both Waste Disposal and Wod were banking on the protection of the letter of the law—nominalism—in the event that there were an eventual lawsuit. "We followed the law in every respect."

But both Waste Disposal and Wod also knew that the law they were obeying was flawed. They knew that this was the reason for the extensive hearings on Capitol Hill. They knew that at any moment the regulations would be drastically altered. They were living on the line, gambling. They gambled that they could complete their project as it was designed before the legislation was finalized into law. The gamble paid off. The project was completed two years before the legislation finally became law.

Does that mean everything is okay?

THE JOURNAL OF MOSES LEVI: JUNE 30, 1987

I have thought a lot about this. Our system of American jurisprudence is somehow flawed. 2204 people contracted cancer that under normal circumstances would not have (according to statistical tables). Of these 1502 died. Fifteen hundred human souls died of the gas emitted from the death chambers created by Waste Disposal and Wod Chemical.

And I defended these bastards. It is as if I had become one of the Nazi Death Camp commandants sending innocent Jews to their death. Yet I, a Jew, have done the same thing! By indirect commission I let the bastards walk. I did not set out to be a bastard myself. I thought I was following all of the rules. I learned them all in law school: the American system of jurisprudence is based upon the principle that all men are innocent until proven guilty. Therefore, the attorney must accept this presumption in his or her defense of the client. You are not the one entitled to pass judgment upon your client. You must act as the client's advocate. You must presume your client's innocence—even if you believe such a presumption to be false. Unless you have physical, empirical evidence (which must be turned over to the court since you are an officer of the court), then you must suppress any suspicions that you have in order to provide your client with the best possible defense to which all presumed innocent persons are entitled.

THE JOURNAL OF MOSES LEVI: JULY 1, 1987

I don't know the hell what I am doing.

They say that Gandhi when he was a lawyer in South Africa never agreed to "get a client off" who he firmly believed to be guilty. Gandhi said that he would seek for the most lenient punishment but would not agree to work for the acquittal of a person he firmly believed to be guilty. Was Gandhi a model lawyer or one who violated the codes of legal ethics?

I don't know why Moses never mentioned any of this to me. I might have acted differently when he approached me to help him with his project. I mean, it isn't philosophy, but I am moved when I read these passages. It connects me with the Moses Levi who I knew at Pembroke.

CHAPTER THREE

The Pembroke Story

Setting the Scene: 1970

PEMBROKE COLLEGE is located in Minnesota about forty miles south of the Twin Cities of Minneapolis and St. Paul. It was founded in 1850 and from its inception was always a co-educational institution. Geographically, Pembroke has a rather more undulating landscape that is generally found in central Minnesota. The college itself is partially surrounded by a large, wooded arboretum. Pembroke originally was located in one building. Students bordered with people from the town. The next two buildings that were built became significant in Pembroke's history. The first was an observatory that had the best telescope west of the Appalachians. The second was the chapel that was to be rebuilt three times (each time getting larger).

The significance of these two buildings was key to Pembroke. In the first case, it created a profitable revenue stream that allowed the college to expand and hire the very best teachers. This revenue stream was created because of the accuracy of the telescope. It permitted the college to sell extremely accurate time calculations to the railroads for whom constant time corrections were essential in order to run an efficient business. This was in the era in which even the best of timepieces needed daily supervision.

The second building enabled the school (in the tradition of many Protestant colleges of the era) to be able offer daily chapel and religious instruction to nurture both the mind and the soul. As such, the chapel lent an air of respectability—very necessary for a school that allowed women as well as men into its doors.

Later, during the early pre-World War I era of the Twentieth Century, Pembroke was one of the first colleges to freely allow Jews and African Americans to matriculate in an integrated fashion. In short, it was considered a radical institution.

Over the years Pembroke maintained a very high reputation. Since small colleges in America before World War II were largely judged in terms of: 1. Money, 2. Old money, and 3. Eastern old money, Pembroke was at a disadvantage. This was compounded by the fact that they were so bent on being a progressive institution. This mission fostered leaders in the Farm Labor Party (later to become the Democratic Farm Labor Party), the Northern League (a Socialist agrarian movement), and a hodgepodge of other Leftist organizations. In this way Pembroke was out of step with the nation. Those who were its advocates thought that it was out of step in just the right way. Those who were its detractors said that it did not pay sufficient respect to money and to old money (such as it existed in Minnesota in those days).

Those on the East Coast felt that the rest of the country was one big cow pasture, desert, or mountain. Those who were capable made it in the East. Those who couldn't make it in the East headed West and stopped at the appropriate place. Thus the United States of America could be read as a scale of decreasing competence beginning at the East Coast and devolving westward.

So it was that even in 1970 when Moses Levi and Peter Simon applied to college that almost all of the best small colleges were thought to be in the East. Only Pembroke in the Midwest and Pomona in Southern California were exceptions.

Given this, why did Moses and Peter apply to Pembroke? In Moses' case it was because his older brother went to Pembroke. He had studied science and graduated highly in his class. After college, Moses' brother got his Ph.D. from the University of Chicago in Physics. However, his mistake was finishing in only four years. As such his student deferment ran out and he was drafted into the Army to fight in Vietnam. Because of his education, he was given a commission and assigned to a command center near Saigon. In the third month of his tour of duty, Moses' brother was killed in a missile barrage upon the center. This tragedy occurred during Moses' last year of high school.

It seemed to Moses that he had to follow in his brother's footsteps and retrieve the mantle that had been wrested from his brother so abruptly.

Peter sought out Pembroke for two reasons. The first was that Peter had been born in the Midwest. He had been forced to move because of his father's job in 1962. They moved to New Jersey in a rural area in the midst of the Watchung Mountains. Then after a couple of years they moved again. This time they headed out to Seattle and lived in the city, at the bottom of Queen Anne Hill on West Mercer Street. Peter was rather confused by all of this. He possessed a great advantage and disadvantage: he was an outsider. Into this void, Peter met Harry Emory.

Harry was eighty-five when Peter became his friend. Emory had been a Pembroke graduate of '03. Then he served in a South Dakota high school (Hancock High School) for fifty years, first as an English teacher and then as the principal (twenty-five years). Harry was married to Lois, his wife of forty-two years, but had never had any children of his own. Instead, Harry's study was filled with photographs of all the boys and girls who had been his students over the years. Harry kept a card file with all of their names and their time at Hancock, their connection to him, the courses they had taken, the dates of those courses, the grades they had received, and the correspondence history since graduation. Harry had no biological children, but he had hundreds of former students.

Peter immediately took to Harry and so it was no wonder that Peter applied to Pembroke for college.

Moses came to Pembroke from a high school that was touted to be the best high school in Milwaukee: Milwaukee Tech. Peter came to Pembroke from a high school that was rather poor. It was so mediocre that Peter ended up having to teach himself if he was to get anything out of high school.

CHAPTER FOUR

The Pembroke Story

September 19, 1970

IT WAS EIGHT O'CLOCK in the morning. The key went into the lock. In the room was an eighteen-year-old boy asleep in his underwear on a bed that had no sheets. The room was askew with furniture. One of the bigger pieces, a chest of drawers, had been propped against the door.

The key turned the lock, but nothing happened.

"Let me try that," barked a man's voice.

The key went in again. It turned all the tumblers and then the knob twisted. But the door didn't open. Then there were a series of pounding sounds as the man put his shoulder to the door. The door and the chest of drawers moved about three inches. Because of the position of the bed (sandwiched between the chest of drawers and a small desk--all against the door), it was rather difficult for the man in the hall to make any significant progress. However, a mighty effort might have toppled the chest of drawers onto the boy who was just entering the world of wakefulness.

"Damn it all," said the man. "Somebody has blocked the door." Then the man rapped his fist on the door. "Who's in there? Open up. Open up the door this instant!"

The figure on the bed stirred. He turned his gaze toward the three-inch crack in the doorway. What he saw was the feathered tip of a woman's hat. A woman's hat. That was it. He rolled out of bed and fell to the floor, letting out a groan as he fell onto his injured right knee.

More knocks. "Open up."

"Please. Stop," said the underwear-clad boy on the floor.

These were the first words that the parents heard. It was at that moment that Moses intervened. "Someone's in there," Moses said.

"Of course someone's in there," replied his father.

"Maybe it's my roommate," Moses said.

"No. The dormitories don't open up until today. It was in the flyer they sent home. Don't forget that I know all about Pembroke, Moses." But the father's words seemed to catch in his throat even as Moses instinctively put his arm around his father. Moses' mother moved back. She had ceased to be an active agent in this drama.

"Just give me a second," cried the voice from inside the room. "I've got to get my pants on."

Everyone was stationary. There was a scraping sound of moving furniture.

The door opened. A tall, skinny, curly hair boy with acne appeared dressed in a tee shirt and jeans.

"Who are you?" asked the man in a defiant manner.

"My name is Peter Simon from Seattle," said the boy.

"Humph," replied the man. Then his wife strode forward, "Peter, you are Moses' roommate. Sorry to have awoken you so early, but we can only stay until ten and we've got to get our boy moved in."

Peter shook the woman's hand and gestured that he was ready to let things happen.

"You know I'm Jewish," said Moses. The two boys were lying in the bunks. Moses was on the top and Peter was on the bottom. The bunks were made of metal with wire-linked mesh that acted as a box spring. The room was very small with barely enough room for two small desks, two chests of drawers, and a tiny closet. It was an engineering marvel to fit so much into so small an area.

"So what?" replied Peter. He stared at the dial of the clock radio that had been his high school graduation present.

"Nothing. I just wanted you to know."

"Why? I mean, I like chocolate ice cream. Is that something you should know? Does that make a difference?"

"My brother said—"

"What did your brother say?"

"My brother said that you should always tell people that you are Jewish."

"Why? Are you bragging or complaining?"

"Neither. Truth in advertising, I suppose."

"Truth in advertising. What is this? Am I buying you?"

"Shut up."

"Sure, but you were the one to bring up the topic."

The boys didn't say anything for a time. The light was gone. It was already ten o'clock. Peter said, "Say, you know I've got this clock radio and it can get rock stations."

"Really?"

"Sure. If you like, I can spin the dial and we can listen to some tunes while we go to sleep."

"Sounds good to me."

And that was the beginning of a nightly ritual that lasted for the rest of their time together—that is whenever they went to bed at the same time (which became an ever decreasingly common event).

* * *

Floor party. This was what the sign said. Peter copied the information and discussed it with Moses at dinner. Whatever else happened, Moses and Peter always ate dinner together.

At Pembroke there were several dining options. There was "Burton" that represented the most efficient service (meaning that you got your food the fastest), but the quality was the lowest. Then there was "Goodhue" which was popular with the boys because there were a lot of good-looking girls in Goodhue. Then there was "Evans," the best food on campus but in a cramped setting (however lots of leaded glass windows that provided a great view). Finally, there was "Severance." Severance was a mahogany paneled room with medallion-plastered ceilings. It was like an Old World treasure. In Severance, you sat at a table and were served by student waiters on work contracts. Everyone ate "family style" (meaning that a dish with a heap of potatoes, beans or whatever was placed in the center of the table and passed around).

As freshmen, Moses and Peter began eating at Burton and later moved to Severance.

"So what's a floor party?" asked Moses.

"I don't know. But they said that attendance was mandatory."

"What are they going to do? Expel us?"

"Well, I'm going. I don't know about you."

Moses began coughing on some undercooked peas.

* * *

The site for the party was in the arboretum. There was a baseball-sized field that figured as a clearing in a large forest. The floor party was really a 4-floor party—two all boys floors and two all girls floors. At the floor party, Moses and Peter picked up plastic cups and poured themselves some beer. For both boys it was the first beer they had ever tasted. The keg was placed near the woods where a couple games of Frisbee began. The two boys stood together trying bravely to consume their beer.

Then a girl in a tie-dyed tee shirt approached them. She was from third floor Norse (an all girls dormitory). "Hey, where's the beer?"

Moses pointed. The keg was only five feet away. The girl poured herself a half glass and returned to the pair. "Do you guys like to Frisbee?"

"No," said Moses and Peter in unison.

The girl laughed. "What are you, twins?"

"No. First cousins," said Peter immediately. "Can't you see the resemblance?"

The girl cocked her head.

Moses laughed. "What's your name?"

"Jill," she said, suddenly shy. The wind blew her long blond straight hair into her eyes. She pretended to be irritated.

"Well, I'm Peter and this is my cousin, Moses."

"Moses? Like from the Bible?"

"We're both from the Bible, really. Were on temporary furlough. Do you want to walk with us and achieve salvation?"

Jill looked as if she'd just seen her parents! "Oh, no thank you. I think I'll pass. Bye-bye, boys."

And that was that.

Moses dropped his beer. Some of the beer spilled on his blue jeans. "What was that all about?"

"What?"

"Us being brothers."

"Cousins."

"Shit, whatever. And the Bible. I think you've had enough." Then Moses poured Peter's barely consumed cup of beer on the ground.

"Lighten up, boy. We've got a lot of talent scouting ahead of us."

And with that, the two went their separate ways.

*   *   *

"Moses?"

"Yeah. What is it?" The two boys were lying in bed ostensibly reading before dinner.

"I was thinking," began Peter as he lifted his legs from his bed and placed his feet on the bottom of the springs that held his roommate's upper bunk mattress. When Peter pushed upwards he could bounce his roommate into attention. "We need to create a signal system."

"A signal system?"

"Yeah, a signal system. I'll talk to you about it at dinner."

Peter and Moses left early for dinner so that there was hardly a line in Burton. When they had assembled their food, Peter began again about the signal system.

"What are you talking about?" asked Moses as he began crunching his way through Sunday "mystery meat delight."

"Well," began Peter, "say you bring a girl back to the room and you start making out. Then it wouldn't be very cool to have your roommate come into the room at that moment."

"You mean you're having sex?"

"Not necessarily having sex. Not all the way. But you see what I mean. It still could be awkward."

"Not necessarily having sex. But perhaps playing monopoly? Those dice rolls can be intense."

"Look, Moses. This is as much for your benefit as it is for mine. We need a system."

"What do you have in mind?" Moses winced as he bit into some sort of inedible nastiness in mystery meat delight.

"Has to be something simple and inconspicuous. Like a folded piece of paper stuck in the name plate bracket."

"A folded piece of paper stuck in the name plate bracket?" Moses was taking the part of the moron.

"Yeah, if you come by and see the paper there, you turn away."

"Where do I go?"

"Who the hell cares? You go somewhere. Anywhere. Just keep out of the room."

"And all this for monopoly? After all, nobody is having sex, right?"

"You're a stupid twit."

"Sure. But let me get this straight. I bring a girl back to our room and as she strides into the cavernous luxury of our suite, I nonchalantly pick up a folded piece of paper that just happened to be lying on my dresser and proceed to put it into the name plate bracket outside the door. And just in case I haven't brought a total cretin to the room, she's going to ask me what I'm doing. Of course I will say in my most suave voice that I am putting a signal system in place so that we won't be disturbed. And then my female companion will say that it's totally unnecessary unless, of course, I have intentions of taking her pants off, in which case she will make here exit now to save us both the embarrassment of it all.

"Yes, Peter, I think it's an excellent system and should work excellently!"

Then it was Peter's turn to gag on a large piece of grizzle embedded within the mystery meat. Peter took a glass of red liquid that was affectionately called "bug juice" and achieved equilibrium. "Good. I'm glad that issue is settled."

*   *   *

One night about two weeks later, Peter was returning from the library. It was around ten o'clock and the piece of paper was set in the nameplate. Peter was angry. "This is a Wednesday night, damn it all. No one goes out on a Wednesday. It's a night to study." Peter's first instinct was to open the door directly. But he knew that could have serious consequences. Then Peter decided to go outside and see whether he could look inside the room. The room was on the first floor that was raised about twenty feet from the ground, so Peter could see the top third of the room but little else. The nine-foot ceilings allowed for only a few inches of Moses' head. But Moses sported a "white-fro" (meaning an Afro-styled hairstyle on a white boy with tight curly hair). Moses' white-fro would be unmistakable.

Out on the lawn Peter could see into the room. The shades had not been pulled. There was, however, no sign of Moses. This could be because Moses had a girl in the room, but that wasn't very likely. Peter had been seeing several women during the first month of classes, but Moses had not seen a single girl. He had had no dates. Not one. This made Peter very sure that Moses was playing a trick on him. Then Peter saw the top of Moses' head walk across the room. He was moving from his desk to the dressers.

"That's it," thought Peter. "He's just shitting me."

Peter broke into a run and bounded up the steps and turned the doorknob without even trying his key (the door locking system employed a pair of buttons that either locked the door each time it was shut—top button, or kept it open all the time—bottom button). This time the door had been left open as was their general custom when someone was in the room and was not sleeping.

Moses was at his desk working. Moses tilted his head upon Peter's appearance. "Hello, Peter."

"What do you mean putting up our sign when you didn't have a girl in the room?"

Moses cracked a half-smile. "I didn't know that it was ever a stipulation that there had to be a girl in the room."

"What?"

"I thought that we merely said that we might put up the sign when we wanted to avoid embarrassment at the other's entry."

"What the fuck are you talking about?"

"Well, I'm working on my physics lab here and I am doing terribly. I thought it would be better if I were alone so that if I broke down there would be no witness."

"Moses. You know I go to sleep around eleven and I need some time to unwind. This is totally unreasonable. Besides, you also know that I suggested this as a device for bringing girls to the room."

"But I have no girls to bring to the room. If there is a system for the convenience of one, then it should be expanded so that it exists for the convenience of two. If you choose to use it for girls, then so be it. If I use it so that I might be alone in my failure, then that should be my right."

Peter shut the door and dropped his books on his desk. He said to himself, "This guy's got it all wrong to follow his brother in physics. He ought to be a lawyer."

*   *   *

As the term moved past Halloween toward Thanksgiving, Moses began to show definite signs of unraveling. The mid-term grades had been rather poor for Moses. In German (a subject that Moses had taken in high school and which he also knew because of the Yiddish spoken in his household), Moses had gotten a B+. In math and physics, Moses had failed the mid-term test. (Pembroke was on the trimester system in which a student only took three classes a term.)

Peter, on the other hand, had an A in French, an A in Philosophy, and a B+ in English.

After dinner one night the boys returned to their room to study. It was Friday night and each of them had a test the next week.

The two boys entered the room, kicked off their shoes and arranged their books. Peter shifted his weekly work schedule so that he could see what he planned to accomplish. (Peter set this up in hourly grids.)

Moses sat at his desk and sharpened a pencil. Then he sharpened another pencil, making sure that the shavings made it into his wastebasket. Moses opened his textbook, picked up one pencil and then put it down again.

Moses just couldn't get started. "Peter, I just can't do this."

"Do what?"

"The whole thing."

"What are you talking about?"

"Pembroke. My brother. Everything."

"What does your brother have to do with it?"

"You know. I've told you how successful he was at Pembroke. Physics major. He went to the University of Chicago in Physics—the best program in the world in physics when he went there. Got his Ph.D. On the way to a successful career. Except for Vietnam."

Peter got up and put his hand upon Moses' shoulder, "You're not your brother."

Moses began to cry. He didn't want to cry, but he did anyway. "Tell that to my parents. My brother is dead. My brother was perfect. And now I am failing everything."

Peter knelt down and put his hand to Moses's cheek. "You're a bright guy. You may not be your brother. I'm not my brother. But you work your butt off. No one can demand more of himself than that."

"But it's NOT GOOD ENOUGH!"

"Maybe physics isn't your area? Maybe you should try something else. Just because your brother was in physics doesn't mean you have to be."

Moses regained composure. "It's so easy for you, Peter. You can't understand."

"Maybe I chose classes in which I knew I could succeed. I don't know. You can't judge yourself on what someone else does. That will cut you inside out."

The two boys stared deeply into each other's eyes. Then Moses looked to his physics book. He was ready to try again.

*   *   *

Both boys got final grades that were identical to their midterms. Moses was on a list of individuals on academic probation. Unless he could pass all of his courses in the second term, he was out of Pembroke.

For the second term, Moses chose German 2, Political Science 100, and English Composition. He ended up with a B+, an A and a B, respectively. Peter got an A in French 4, an A in English Composition, and a B+ in Comparative Religion.

*   *   *

The second term at Pembroke was brutal. Because of its location, it was beset with some of the coldest temperatures in the lower forty-eight. This meant that it was not uncommon to have a real air temperature (not a wind chill temperature) of 40 below zero, Fahrenheit.

Both Moses and Peter tried out and made the basketball team. But neither boy played very much. Peter dropped off the team midway through the season while Moses stuck it out until the end. Both the boys also engaged in the unofficial winter sports of a different sort: sledding down the Evans hill on the tray you just ate dinner on; playing snow football; and engaging in mammoth snowball fights that would last for hours.

Peter tried to push his own studying system upon Moses. It was a very structured system that required a person to work according to a time clock. Moses balked at this system and instead began studying later and later into the night. While Peter was always in bed before midnight, Moses often studied all night.

Still, the rituals were maintained. They ate dinner together each day and discussed common problems. When it became time to get a room for the next year, they both were sure that they wanted to room together again. They got a good number in the room lottery and picked up a prime double in Evans with its own private bathroom.

* * *

It was halfway through the fall term of their sophomore year that Peter met Sarah. The two of them had been taking an English literature survey course together (along with thirty others). They were assigned into teams to create bibliographies on various Seventeenth Century writers. Sarah and Peter were assigned to Milton.

"So when do you want to do this?" asked Sarah right after class.

"Do you think we can do it at one sitting? Shouldn't we break it up some?"

"Well, we don't really know anything, do we, until we go over and open up the Cambridge Bibliography of English Literature."

"Okay. You name the time," suggested Peter.

"This afternoon," said Sarah.

"Can't this afternoon. How about the evening, say around seven?"

"Let's make it eight. I'll meet you at the reference desk."

*   *   *

When they departed, Peter began to see Sarah in a different way. She was not what you would call a beautiful girl. If you looked at her features individually, each one was lacking in some way. Her shoulder length black hair was too frizzy. Her nose was too big. Her chin was too sharp. Her brown eyes weren't soft, but glowed with intensity. Her complexion was still suffering from puberty. But there was something about the whole that Peter found attractive.

That evening Peter arrived a half-hour early. Sarah was already there.

"I thought you had something at seven so that's why you chose eight," said Peter.

"No. I chose eight because *you* suggested seven and I didn't want to give in too easily."

"No. I don't like a girl who's too *easy*," said Peter with a smile.

Sarah screwed up her face, half-smiling, half-exasperated. The two held their gaze for longer than either meant to. They also studied longer than either had intended. They were still in the main reading room at midnight when it closed.

Peter walked Sarah back to her dorm. She was staying on that weird 4th Meyers floor. ("Hey, I'm a freshman, I don't have much choice.") The moon was still out and the chill of autumn brought a freshness to the air.

Meyers was only a couple hundred yards from the library, but the two lingered outside the door, their words billowed like clouds in the cold night air.

And then Peter was alone.

*   *   *

The next morning, Moses had to shake his roommate awake. "Get-up, lazy head. If you're going to stay out till two, then you have to buck up like a man."

Peter threw his pillow at Moses. It missed and knocked some books onto the floor. "Roll out, Peter. You can't afford to miss any more eight o'clock French classes."

Eight a.m. classes were an invention of the Devil to try the souls of men. Peter was generally up in time (going to bed before midnight), but Peter did not start the day quickly. Early afternoon was his best time.

This morning was especially difficult. All Peter could think about was Sarah Wolfe (who also went by Sarah Z.—after her middle name, Zipporah). There must be some way that he could run into her so that he wouldn't have to wait until tomorrow at class to see her again.

Another shake. Moses was fulfilling his duty—and then some, as he roughed up his semi-somnolent companion.

A cup of cold coffee, a handful of leftover popcorn and Peter was ready to face the world—sort of.

*   *   *

After his two morning classes, Peter decided to take a turn in the tunnels. The tunnels were an underground series of paths that were constructed so that the heating pipes would be accessible for repair. They also served another useful purpose during the cold months. They connected most of the campus underground. In this way, a student could walk across campus and not have to brave the bitter cold. A person could (given the right schedule) spend days at a time in a tee shirt and sandals even while wind chills of sixty below zero swept across the world above.

During the fall and late spring it was rare to find students in the tunnels. They were too hot and stuffy. So it was that at these times of the year the tunnels provided a perfect recluse where a person could shuffle in and out of the light and shadows created by the intermittent string lighting.

On the walls were various forms of intellectual graffiti ranging from "Si fractus illabatur orbis, Impavidum ferient ruinae!" to "Candy is dandy, but sex don't hurt your teeth." Peter shuffled forward. His hands were thrust deeply into his pockets and he was hunched over. All of a sudden he heard a noise. Peter slid into a shadow and watched as another figure turned the corner from an adjoining tunnel. He couldn't believe his eyes. He couldn't believe his luck. The figure turning the corner was Sarah.

"Sarah."

The figure stopped. From out of the shadows emerged a form. She couldn't believe her eyes. She couldn't believe her luck. The figure was Peter.

"Peter. What are you doing down here?"

"You know, I was going to ask you the same thing."

The two were now standing in front of each other, separated by only inches.

Sarah tried to say something but she could only sigh.

"Come on," said Peter taking Sarah's hand. "Let's go back to my room and talk."

"Okay," said Sarah.

When they got to the room, Peter unlocked the door and bid Sarah sit on the couch. (The Evans room was much bigger than Peter's freshman room.) Then Peter turned and picked up a slip of paper from atop his dresser and inserted it in the outside nameplate before shutting the door.

"What was that?" asked Sarah.

"Oh just a message for my roommate in case he drops by this afternoon," replied Peter walking over to the couch.

"You leave messages for each other?"

"Let's not talk about my roommate," said Peter, sitting down right next to Sarah. "I find *you* much more interesting."

Sarah smiled and gazed into Peter's eyes. "You know, Peter. Sometimes people communicate better without any words at all."

CHAPTER FIVE

The Pembroke Story

Spring Term, 1972

IT WAS MAY DAY. Spring midterms were in progress, and winter was largely over (though relapses often occurred). Moses got up from his desk to look out his window onto Evans Field. It was a large grassy field that could support as many as four softball games at once. Nobody was playing ball just now, but the verdant beauty of the scene brought Moses a sense of peace. The field was virtually vacant--just a guy flying a kite and a couple on a stroll, too far away to detect.

In a few weeks he would have to declare a major. Peter had already decided upon philosophy. Moses was torn between political science and philosophy. It was a bittersweet decision for Moses since he really couldn't feel success at either. That feeling of accomplishment had been reserved for physics (a field he knew now he'd never master). His grades had been good in both political science and in philosophy—though slightly better in political science. However, he liked philosophy more.

It was a difficult choice. Moses' father was a pharmacist. He had really wanted to be a research scientist, but he didn't have the money for more than junior college. In those days before World War II, it was tough financing a college education. When the war came, he was newly married with a child on the way. His specialized knowledge allowed him to work at a stateside dispensary. After the war there was no time to think about going back to school. At thirty-two he had to go about the business of supporting his family. Gert Levi (short for Gershom) was a hardworking man who was also a no-nonsense kind of guy. He had constructed blinders to anti-Semitism, believing his strength and determination could overcome any obstacle. Gert tried to instill his intensity into his two boys. Without a war and a young child to interrupt their quest for the Promised Land, perhaps they could realize in their lives what had only been an unfulfilled dream in his own.

Would Gert understand Moses' choice? Whenever Moses went back to Milwaukee on break, his father would go into this speech about how Moses had gotten off to a rocky start when he first attended Pembroke. Everyone had a rocky patch at times. Why, there had been the time when they had been denied the ability to buy a house in a certain neighborhood because of a covenant against Jews in the neighborhood association. And then there had been the time that the War had interrupted his Dream. These things happen. But maybe Moses could get back to those science classes now that he was getting comfortable at Pembroke. Maybe he could give it another try.

So Moses gave it another try. He enrolled in another math class and failed it. So much for Gert's theory. Why couldn't his father accept him for what he *was* good at instead of holding out The Dream for him to gaze at?

The sunny field drew Moses's attention but he knew that he had a lot of studying to do for his remaining mid-term. No matter how hard he tried, it always seemed to him that he had to study twice as hard as Peter did and end up with a lower grade.

None of this seemed very fair. Why should philosophy come so easy to Peter? Peter picked up the math and the logic that were at the core of philosophy. He could reconstruct the logical arguments in a quarter of the time that it took Moses. Why?

It would be one thing to take a long time, but then to be able to feel that at the end of it, a better product was attained. But how does one understand taking a longer time to only attain parity (if he was lucky) with his roommate? It seemed as if Peter were gifted in such a way that was cosmically unfair. First, there was Peter's eye-brain interaction that allowed him to read twice as fast as Moses. That is something one is born with. No matter how much broccoli he ate or how many eye exercises he did, Moses would always read more slowly than Peter. This was a natural disadvantage that Moses did not deserve. The flip side to this is that Peter had a natural advantage in this respect that he, also, did not deserve.

Second, there was the fact that Peter's dad had been a salesman. At the family dinner table there were lively debates between a master of persuasion (Peter's dad) and the rest of the family. This had to have been a great break for Peter. It helped him argue and persuade others. It helped him garner second place in his state's National Forensic League Tournament (gaining Peter the double ruby debate classification).

Moses, on the other hand, often ate dinner with only his mother since his father worked long hours at the pharmacy and his brother was generally engaged in some sort of "super genius" science program. Moses and his mother discussed school, books they were reading, and what was happening to their friends. It was a low-key affair, not very efficacious at honing the critical debating skills necessary for philosophy.

Thus, in the second place, Peter had a home environment that nurtured skills that helped him move through the argumentative structure more easily. This was due to an environmental effect that was out of his control: the home situation that his parents provided for him. Since it was out of his control, he did not deserve the good effects that such an environment provided him. Likewise, Moses did not deserve the lack of such skills that *could have been provided to him* had his home environment been different.

The list could go on. But the same sort of dynamics would occur. Many of the most important skills that were necessary for success were either due to nature or to nurture. None of these were in the control of the agent, ergo, the agent is not deserving for their acquisition nor is he deserving for their absence. If possession of these attributes and skills is necessary for success, then much of one's success is undeserved. It is rather the consequence of luck or good fortune.

The couple. Moses now saw the couple on the field. It was Peter and Sarah. They were walking hand-in-hand, talking as only lovers can. Behind the glass, Moses focused his gaze upon the pair. The wide expanse of the field had become a narrow tunnel.

Moses held his hands together tightly so that the whites of his knuckles showed from under his skin. He wanted to turn back to continue his work but he could not break his gaze. Moses followed with his eyes as they crossed the field toward Evans' hill. His gaze was locked upon the couple until they were completely out of view.

CHAPTER SIX

The Pembroke Story

Fall Term, 1973

IT WAS EARLY OCTOBER at Pembroke. The leaves were very vibrant in their yellows and reds. Sarah Z. was walking around the Bell Lakes that guarded the entrance to both Goodhue and the Arboretum. Sarah was just beginning her junior year in college. The recently declared English major had a book of poetry in one hand. She intended to read it in the woods.

It was a beautiful day. The temperature was around 75 degrees Fahrenheit and there was just the slightest breeze in the air.

Sarah couldn't help wondering whether life would have been different had she been accepted to the London Program, too. Peter and Sarah had applied last April for the program that put you right in London for a term studying with a Pembroke professor who made the trip with the team and taught the required two classes necessary to maintain matriculation status. (And then the professor stayed the rest of the year in London on sabbatical.) There were also opportunities to take classes at the University of London as well as to intern at various EU offices located in London. It sounded like a great program to Sarah.

Peter made it in (he seemed to lead such a charmed life). Sarah did not make it in. This made Sarah quite despondent. She had been dating Peter steadily since her freshman year. They weren't officially "engaged" because this wasn't something that Pembroke students did until just before graduation (if at all). But they were serious about each other and parted with an "understanding." The exact nature of the understanding was rather vague (as most understandings are), but did revolve around a notion that the two of them would pick up where they left off once Peter came back for his final two terms at Pembroke come January 10th.

Peter had written Sarah just one letter in the month he'd been away. It gave some news on the program, the plays he was seeing and all the tremendous lectures he was able to attend in London (as well as in Oxford and Cambridge). It seemed like a very stimulating experience.

Sarah reached the woods and found a nice soft spot to sit down next to a vine maple whose leaves were fully yellow. The canopy of leaves provided just the right amount of filtering so that she could read. The book she had was *The Collected Poems of John Keats.* It seemed like the right kind of book to read in the middle of the woods on an autumn afternoon.

But try as she might, Sarah could not concentrate on the elevated sentiments of Keats. Her "negative capability" wasn't working. All she could think about was Peter. He was such a success in everything he attempted. Peter was the only philosophy student at Pembroke ever to get an article accepted for publication in a peer-reviewed journal of philosophy. He wrote an essay on number theory and Frege.

On the basis of that essay and his GRE scores that Peter had taken in the spring, The University of Chicago had already accepted him as a Ph.D. student, even before he had begun his senior year in college. Everyone used adjectives such as, "brilliant," "gifted," and "genius" to describe Peter. One had the feeling around campus that everyone eyed Peter in such a way that they were expecting to be asked thirty years from now whether they actually knew Peter and what they thought of him.

In a school of nerds and overachievers, Peter Simon was the golden boy destined for greatness. Sarah Z. had been the girlfriend of the golden boy. This was an interesting position, actually. To be the girlfriend of the golden boy meant that all of your friends saw you through a lens. The lens had the distortion imprinted upon it, "This is the girlfriend of the golden boy." Everything that she did and everyone that she met saw her as mediated through Peter.

Sarah Z. loved Peter. He was a great intellect and a kind person. What more could a girl ask for? This was a question that she often asked herself for the inevitable time that Peter would ask her to marry him: "What more could a girl ask for?"

It was a difficult question. Sarah Z. tried putting the question to G.E. Moore's Open Question Test (that Peter had detailed to her at great length one evening), but it didn't seem to work. Did this mean that philosophy couldn't answer questions about real life, or did it simply mean that Sarah didn't know how to apply the Open Question Test?

While Sarah Z. was contemplating this disjunct, a shadow came over her. She looked up. It was Moses Levi, Peter's roommate.

"All alone in solitary confinement?" asked Moses.

Sarah didn't answer but tried to focus on the face that was somewhat obscured by the back lighting of the sun.

"Mind if I sit down?" asked Moses.

"It's a free country," replied Sarah.

"Is it?" said Moses as he sat on some leaves across from Sarah. "Sometimes I wonder."

Moses sat akimbo while Sarah had her legs straight out, using the tree as back support. "So have you heard from Peter?" asked Sarah.

"Yes, I got a short note. Peter's not much of a letter writer—at least not to me, I guess."

"No. Not to me either. Saves his brain cells for all that philosophy that he," Sarah Z. paused a moment, "—and you, of course. The both of you. I mean, ah. Well, I guess I don't know what I mean."

"I know what you mean. And thank you."

Sarah Z. smiled and proceeded to talk until dinnertime with Moses about Peter. The conversation hadn't finished so the two went over to Severance (the up-scale family-style dining hall) to conclude their conversation.

*   *   *

But the conversation didn't stop there. The next morning, Moses planted himself upon a sculpture just outside of Watson Hall where Sarah Z. lived in a single so that if she exited the dormitory, anytime after 8:30 Sunday morning, Moses would see her and be able to say, "Sarah Z.! Funny meeting you like this." Such was the plan.

At 11:00 am Moses began to speculate on how long he would wait for Sarah Z. He had work with him that could last until noon.

The dining halls opened for lunch at 11:15 and closed at 1:00. On Sundays they were very strict about this.

Then Moses felt a tap on his shoulder. He jerked suddenly and dropped his book (he almost fell off of the bench in front of the sculpture).

"I didn't mean to scare you," said the voice. It was Sara Z!

"Where did you come from?" said Moses, unable to control his reaction.

"From my mother and father by the grace of God," replied Sarah Z.

"No, you misunderstand me," started Moses before he thought better of revealing his plan.

"Oh, so you want to know my schedule, do you? I didn't pick that up from our conversation yesterday."

"I didn't know who I was yesterday. I mean—" Moses stopped. He had no further subterfuges in him. He spoke without reflection. "Yesterday—"

"Yes?" Suddenly Sarah Z. felt as if she were in control. Moses was in *her* power.

"Yesterday was the beginning of the rest of my life."

"Oh my, we are dramatic."

Moses, who had just retrieved his book, dropped it a second time. The soft cover tome on Locke, Berkeley, and Hume would not accept the physical jarring of another tumble. As quickly as he could, Moses' mind was scrambling. He was not a quick thinker, but somehow he was able to look up to Sarah Z. and say, "Do you like mystery meat?"

"I beg your pardon?" was her reply.

"Mystery meat. Pembroke's Sunday night fare. Haven't you always hated it?"

"I hadn't given it much thought, really. Why do you ask?"

"Well, I suggest that we go out to Dave's tonight."

"Dave's?" replied Sarah Z.

"Yeah. Haven't you ever been to Dave's before? I can't believe that—"

"Of course, I've been to Dave's for their pizza. But I'm not really in the mood for pizza."

"Dave's has more than pizza. They also have fried chicken. And beer, too."

"You like beer?" asked Sarah Z.

"Not that much. I always had it with Peter because I know how much *he* likes beer."

Sarah Z. laughed. "You know it's the same with me. I don't like beer much, either. But I drank it with Peter because he was such a fan."

"Peter's gone," said Moses. "We don't have to be just as we were with Peter."

Sarah Z put her arms around Moses' head and gave him a short kiss on the lips. "You're right, Moses. I feel liberated. Let's go out to eat at Dave's tonight."

Moses beamed.

"Dutch, of course," added Sarah Z.

"Of course."

CHAPTER SEVEN

Peter Simon

July 10, 2000

THE JOURNAL OF MOSES LEVI:
JULY 2, 1987

 I figure that I earned about $1,400,000 in fees working on the Waste Disposal case. I won the case. My peers said, "What a great strategy." I earned an additional bonus from my firm. They made a lot of money, too. But they never said, "Justice has been done!"
 What of the 1502 victims of Waste Disposal's actions?
 What of my actions to deflect the true course of justice?
 My fee. Is it blood money?

I GOT A CALL around seven-thirty in the morning. That is rather rude. It was the FBI. I guess they don't give a damn about being rude.
 "Peter Simon?"
 "Ugh. Who are you? Who calls at this hour?"
 "This is the **F. B. I.** "
 "So what?
 "This is the **F. B. I.**"
 "What do you want *me* to do about it?"
 "An agent will be by your house in fifteen minutes," he said as the doorbell rang.
 I got out of bed and made my way to the door. I generally sleep in pajamas but since Monique left I have stopped doing laundry on a

regular basis. This means that my two pairs of pajamas were not clean and I slept in my underwear.

I wondered if it was Monique coming back to me. I started thinking of a series of harangues that I could level against her. Why did you leave so suddenly? Did you ever hear of leaving somebody a note? I mean really, I took care of you for almost three years while you explored you inner being. What am I? Just a sugar daddy who gives you a place to crash?

I was already waking up in anticipation of what I'd say to her.

Then I opened the door to a blonde uniformed woman with a huge gun at her side. Her hair was pulled up tight against her skull. She had perfect bone structure and pale white skin. When she saw me she didn't alter one facial muscle. "Mr. Simon?"

"What?" I began, hastily trying to recoup. I do consider myself to be a rather enlightened man, but I did not fancy standing in my jockeys in front of a total stranger—especially a female stranger.

I tried to shut the door on her, but the strong arm of the law intervened and before I knew it, I was on the ground with the blonde on top of me. Under normal circumstances the prospect of being clad only in my underwear underneath a blonde woman all dressed up as a policewoman would be rather stimulating to me. But in this circumstance I didn't think the situation would really lead to something that I would enjoy.

I was right. The amazon twisted me over and handcuffed me from behind before I knew it. Just like those calf-roping contests, she had me down and delivered in no more than twenty seconds.

"You're going downtown, asshole," she said.

"In that case can I put on some pants?"

This seemed to catch her by surprise. The fact that someone might actually dislike parading around all of Washington, DC in his jockey briefs never occurred to her.

After a very long interval (during which my face was pressed to the floor under the force of her steel grip), she said, "All right. I suppose that's okay, but I'll put on your pants, myself." She barked out each word as if it came from a voice synthesizer machine.

This was a daydream gone totally wrong. Fräulein Gestapo was a sadist with a single purpose on her mind. I waited in dread at how she might execute her task.

She pushed me into various rooms before hitting on my bedroom. It never occurred to her to ask me first. Why miss all the fun? With each try there was a decided shove that generally meant I went to the floor.

Then I was yanked up from behind and we began again. When we finally reached the right room, she pulled some pants from my #1 pile. (In the interests of efficiency, I often put my clothes into three piles. #1 pile is "really not that dirty and can be worn again." #2 pile is "a little iffy." #3 pile is "definitely ready for the washer.") She gathered up the legs so that I might step into each hole. Then she raised them briskly, stopping at the crotch. She placed her hand firmly upon the family jewels and finished the job: all up and zipped. The hand lingered a moment as she sneered at me.

What could I do? My hands were cuffed behind my back.

My power lady told me to slide into my slippers because she wasn't about to tie my shoes. Pants and slippers on—check. Time for the ride downtown. I know it was summer. And summer in Washington, DC is rather hot to say the least. Still, I would have appreciated the opportunity to have had a shirt to wear, and perhaps a belt and socks. The whole thing seemed a bit much.

When I was properly seated in an interrogation room, the door was closed and I was alone. It was a rather ordinary room painted pea green with a brown linoleum floor. The walls were bare, save for a prominent mirror. Probably a two-way mirror for the peanut gallery. The ceiling had recessed florescent tube lighting that made everything seem a little too bright.

I waited an hour or more until Henry Hoover made his appearance. He was accompanied by Fräulein Gestapo, who had let down her hair in the interval. Fräulein carried a tape recorder and was the go-between entre the mirror et moi. Who was behind the mirror? A video tape recorder probably. I wasn't important enough for an audience.

"Now, Mr. Simon," began Hoover.

"Dr."

"Excuse me?"

"Dr. Simon, if you please. I have a Ph.D. in philosophy from the University of Chicago which was, when I attended, one of the most prestigious places to study philosophy in the *world*."

Henry laughed. "Okay, *Dr.* Simon." It was all a joke to him.

"Don't take it lightly, young man. I'm sure that you probably have a bachelor's degree from some no-name state university."

"I do not."

"No degree, then, or at least one that you won't own up to? You know, Plato said that evil springs from ignorance. You are a living testimonial to the truth of Plato—just like Fräulein Nazi there—who for the record, since I know you are recording all this behind the mirror, sexually harassed me in her arrest. I would like an opportunity to fill out a complaint form."

Fräulein Nazi leaped from her chair across the table at me, but I slid back. "It's all on film, Fräulein. The end of your career is being run before you. Go ahead and hurt me some more. That way I can have your job *and* Henry's."

This didn't go over so good. Henry got up and waved his hands at the mirror as if to say, 'stop the cameras.' Then he turned and motioned to Fräulein Nazi. The two of them left the room.

I waited another hour before Henry returned alone.

"You caused quite a stir," said the young agent, flexing his biceps.

"This is all totally illegal, you know," I replied.

Hoover slammed his hands flat upon the table. He was livid. "Murder is also illegal, buster. Excuse me, Dr. Buster." Hoover's voice was as loud as he could make it. Instantly, he turned towards the mirror and then looked back to me. "Now we can do this the hard way or the easy way."

"Are you charging me with a crime?" I replied.

Hoover frowned.

"Please answer me. I am entitled to know whether I am being charged of a crime."

Hoover started pacing. "What do you have to hide?"

"Am I being charged of a crime?" I asked.

"You know I can break every bone in your face?"

"I'm quite certain of that. But if you do, you will lose your job and face serious time in jail. Is that what you want?"

Hoover slammed the walls and left. Another hour or so passed by.

Finally, an older woman in a very expensive navy suit came in along with Henry Hoover. The woman must have been seventy if she was a day. She was about five-foot-two with petite delicate features.

Her dark hair was streaked with gray and pulled back in a bun. Her skin was thin and tight about her small head. There was an aura of gravitas about her.

"I am from the legal department at the FBI. I will be present at this interrogation."

She delivered her words as if she were the *puthia* at the Temple of Delphi. I nodded. "Then you are here to hear my complaints against the agency concerning brutality, sexual harassment, and habeas corpus infringement."

This was not the way to start. The lady signaled Hoover to leave. In five minutes, I was given a limousine ride home.

*   *   *

The next day, I was called at seven-thirty in the morning. This call said that I was to go downtown and meet with the FBI at noon. I was welcomed to bring my lawyer with me. Since I had not been charged with a crime, the state would not provide me with a lawyer. Besides, the university was supposed to get me a lawyer. When I called the academic vice president, he said that unless the infraction had to do with my professional capacity as a teacher, they would not represent me.

This was ominous. I knew I needed representation. I just didn't want to pay for it. I racked my brain. Who did I know who was a lawyer that I would trust in such a situation? I decided to call my client, Saul Sani.

"You what?"

"Yes, they want to talk to me. And that's not the half of it." I told Saul what had happened. He was dumbfounded. But he liked it.

"Listen. The stuff you asked me to do for Moses was tough. Pure *pro bono*, if you know what I mean. And unfortunately, in our firm, each of the senior partners has to carry his share or get cut out of the dividend distribution at the end of the year. That can amount to a million bucks, I'm telling you. I'm so leveraged you wouldn't believe it. I can't really afford to kiss off a million bucks."

"I know, Saul. I'm sorry, Saul—"

"No. Don't get me wrong. This thing has money written all over it. They have done everything wrong. We've got them by the balls. It's PAYDAY, BABY. Let's take it to the bank."

There was a reason that Saul and I got on so well together.

*   *   *

At noon Saul Sani, dressed in a thousand dollar suit, and myself, Peter Simon, dressed in a Robert Hall one hundred dollar suit, addressed the same older woman (this time dressed in an identical suit except it was black—a subtle fashion statement) and Henry Hoover.

"How do you do, I'm Alice Minkas, associate council for the FBI."

"I'm Saul Sani of Cohen, Potts, and Sani."

"Of course, I have heard of your firm, Mr. Sani. Do you think that we could have a moment to discuss things in another room?"

And so they left. This time I was left with Hoover, who left after five minutes. He had work to do. As opposed to me, right?

After an extended period—less than an hour but more than a half-hour, the two emerged. Ms. Minkas sat down across from me and said, "Your attorney and I have come to a mutual agreement on a settlement of your complaints subject to your really being innocent of the charge of murder."

"Murder?

"Yes. The murder of Moses Levi."

"Moses has been murdered? I knew he was missing. But have you found his body. Is he dead?"

"No, we have not found his body. But a *corpus delicti* is not necessary for a murder conviction."

"And you think *I* killed Moses?"

"The settlement we have structured depends upon the fact that you *didn't* kill Mr. Levi. However, it is the job of this agency to investigate cases that have national significance. And, as you know, the life or death of Mr. Levi certainly has national significance."

I slumped back into my chair. Almost on cue Mr. Henry Hoover came in. He had a tape recorder in hand and an anxious expression on his face.

Hoover placed the tape recorder on the table. Then he looked to Ms. Minkas.

"Turn on the tape recorder, Henry. For the record, there is a mirror behind you that has been making a continuous record of everything that has happened. This is in accordance with the department's policy. It is available to all parties with a demonstrated 'need to know.'"

Henry lifted his head and now pretended to be a professional interrogator instead of the sadistic goon he really was.

"Mister—excuse me *Doctor*," Hoover cleared his throat and composed himself. "Doctor Simon. We have several questions that we wish to pose to you in connection with the death or disappearance of Moses Levi." Hoover looked at me. I looked at Saul. Saul nodded. I nodded.

"Now, Doctor Simon. Given that Mr. Moses Levi is missing or murdered, and given that in murder we generally concentrate upon motive, means and ah—"

"Opportunity," added Ms. Minkas.

"Yes, opportunity. Let us examine your connection to this case. First and most important is motive. We believe that you have ample motive. To begin, is it true that Mr. Moses Levi took your fiancé away from you and married her?"

"No," I said.

"No? Why we have evidence—"

"Listen, you dumb ass. I tried to teach you before to ask the right question. Now you have *not* asked the right question. If you had asked whether Moses stole the woman I had been dating for two years in college while I was away in Europe on a special program, then the answer would be, 'yes.' If you had asked whether this made me mad, then the answer would be, 'yes.' Who wouldn't be mad? If you asked whether I held a grudge of sorts against Moses, then the answer would be, 'yes.' Who wouldn't hold a grudge? I mean, Moses took my girl and never said a thing. 'All is fair in love and war.' I suppose that was his thinking. But I would have never done such a thing. It was a base and unloyal action.

"However, would I kill a person just because he performed a base and unloyal action? You've got to be kidding. In the American Philosophical Association there is the most persuasive character assassination that occurs anywhere. These intellectual dummies perform all sorts of cruelties in the name of academic purity. They seek to rise by pushing others down. In reality they are no better than politicians or businessmen, both of whom I despise."

"Mr.--er. Doctor Simon. Let's return to the issue. There is the issue of motive. First, Moses Levi took the girl you had been serious about in college—"

"—Excuse me. 'Serious about'? What is that supposed to mean? Does it mean that I planned to marry Sarah? Does it mean that I was banging Sarah? Does it mean that I was inconvenienced about trying to find a new piece of ass for my last two terms in college? Does it mean that I was heartbroken and ready to pine away? Does it mean that –"

"Peter, I think agent Hoover gets the idea." Saul turned toward Hoover. "Do you wish to rephrase the question?"

Hoover seemed out of his element again. Alice Minkas stepped forward. "Let's simplify things, Dr. Simon. Were you in any way upset when you returned from Europe to find that Moses Levi was now going steady with the woman who was your steady before you left?"

"Yes."

"Would you describe your level of anger as low, medium, or high?"

"High."

"To whom was your anger directed?"

"At Sarah, naturally. It was her responsibility to shut down the guys who were going to hit on her. I mean, that's what guys do."

"So you held no anger toward Moses?"

"No. I was mad at him. I just told you so. But my primary anger was towards Sarah. If the situations were reversed, I wouldn't have hit on Moses' girl. But if I had, then it would have been her responsibility to stop me."

"Her responsibility?"

"That's right."

"And if Sarah had been the one to go to Europe, would it have been your responsibility to be the one to say, 'no'?"

"Yes."

Alice Minkas grunted. This last bit had nothing to do with the case, but she thought she might be able to catch me in an inconsistency. She thought that if she got me rattled, then I might confess to everything:

killing Moses, the assassination of John Kennedy, and the Johnstown Flood. These people live in such narrow little worlds. It is amazing that they are the ones entrusted with the safety of our country.

"Well, Dr. Simon," began Minkas again. "Let me put my cards on the table. Moses Levi is missing. He has been since July 4th. No one has seen him after July 3rd. His daughter, Miriam, was away for a post-graduation vacation with friends. On Monday, July 3rd he met with three people in the afternoon: first he met with you, Mr. Sani, then he met with the minority leader of the Senate, then he met with the director of Common Action, Joshua Kaplan. All the meetings were in public venues and we have witnesses who attest to Moses leaving each meeting.

"Now what we are trying to determine is what happened to Moses. People just don't disappear!" Alice Minkas was leaning forward as she delivered her lines. This is about as passionate as a person like Minkas ever gets.

"I will agree that physical disappearance violates all known physical laws." I briefly smiled. "However, it does not violate the laws of the major religions of the world. Each of them offers cases of miraculous disappearances by key leaders."

"And do you think that *this* is what happened to Moses?" Alice threw her hands in the air as if she were asking the most rhetorically useless question that could be asked.

"No. I am not a religious man. But I am a man who has studied the religions of the world as a part of my general education. And I find many narratives like this."

"WHAT DOES THIS HAVE TO DO WITH ANYTHING?" asked Minkas as she started to lose it.

"Materially, nothing. It was simply the complete answer to the question you asked. When you ask an 'all possible worlds' question, then one must be prepared to examine every possibility. Don't blame me. You can curse Gottfried Leibniz for that one."

"Who? Is this another associate of Moses Levi?"

"No, ma'am, he was the co-inventor of the calculus. You know, in mathematics. He lived four hundred years ago."

This time Hoover jumped at me. It was all he could take. Hoover had me on the floor in two seconds flat. The veins on the side of his neck were bulging. "Come on, smart ass, stop talking about these dead people and answer the lady's questions."

I could barely talk because he had his forearm over my throat. But still I managed, "I think you were the one who began talking about dead people—or at least *potentially* dead people."

This caused Hoover to slug me in the jaw. Saul and Alice Minkas intervened. They got rid of Hoover. I tried swallowing a glass of water but my jaw hurt very badly. Instinctively, I checked to determine whether I had all my teeth and whether they were all firmly in place. They were.

Still, there was a considerable aching.

Saul intervened. "Can we have a doctor in here?"

Alice was beside herself. "We don't have a staff doctor. I could call an ambulance, if you like."

"Call an ambulance. This man needs medical attention. Look at his jaw."

And that was that.

CHAPTER EIGHT

Peter Simon

July 11, 2000

SAUL WAS IN a very good mood as he drove me home from my short visit in the hospital. My x-ray showed no broken bone, but it had been recorded that I had contusions and abrasions consistent with a good rap to the jaw. I have played some basketball in my time, so that I know what it is like to take a rap to the jaw. It really wasn't such a big deal, but Saul was gloating. Saul is my age with a bald pate bordered with gray patches on the side. Saul stands about 5'6" and wears dark brown horn-rimmed glasses. He almost always has a smile on his face.

"Thank God you're such a smart ass," said Saul. "This will be really nice."

"Glad to be of service, Saul," I replied.

When we got home Saul came in and sat with me at my old oaken kitchen table. I didn't offer him anything to drink. "I've got to tell you, Peter, the case they're building is circumstantial, but it is rather bad. We've got to act proactively."

"What do you mean, Saul?"

"Look," said Saul taking out a yellow legal pad with writing on it. "They are working on motive and opportunity."

"What do you mean?"

"Listen. On the motive side they have the bit about Sarah."

"That's bullshit."

"I know it's bullshit. That's not the point. We've got to get through this. I need you free and clear for a couple of reasons."

"Not the least of which is our friendship."

"Make that three reasons."

I shook my head and motioned for Saul to continue.

"Look at my notes with me. Second is the whole bit that happened at the press conference."

"Are you serious?"

"Look, eighty million Americans saw Moses challenge you to join his crusade. They saw you wiggle waggle and they heard him call you a moral hypocrite if you didn't go along."

"I was sandbagged. You know that."

"I know more than that. Moses was being pressured by Joshua Kaplan at Common Action. Kaplan wanted Moses out of the organization. Kaplan was playing hardball. Moses turned to you as his last hope. He set you up because everyone else he knew had deserted him. You were it, baby."

For once, I didn't have a response.

"Moses humiliated you before a national television audience who saw it on the nightly news. From the FBI's point of view, that is a possible motive." Saul took off his glasses and looked at me. I have never understood this habit of his. He is blind without his glasses. He always puts them back on before he resumes.

"Next, is Moses' meetings with you. It says in his day planner, now in the hands of the FBI, that he met with you on three occasions after that in order to put pressure on you to get some of your consulting clients to join his court case and help with the pending legislation in Congress."

"That's where you come in, Saul."

"Yes, that's where I come in and in order to keep myself clean, I've got to get this out of the way in a hurry. I cannot afford to have my reputation sullied. A good reputation is all a lawyer has. Take that away and I had better retire."

"Come on, Saul. It's not that bad, is it?"

Saul took off his glasses again. "If you are found innocent, then we have a sweet little personal injury suit against the FBI that they have already agreed to settle. But the settlement is contingent upon your being innocent."

"You believe I'm innocent, don't you, Saul?"

"Of course I do. But what I believe doesn't matter. We have to counter these charges with proactive responses."

"I agree. This charade has to end quickly. I'm not as young as I used to be."

"That's not everything," said Saul. "The last point is rather dicey. It seems that Monique, the girl you have been seeing—"

"—Try living with for almost three years."

"All the worse. Monique has been dating a guy from Moses' staff, a fellow named Sam Rodriguez. It seems that she moved in with him on July 3rd."

"The bitch said she was going to be out with friends for the Fourth. Holy shit!"

"Holy shit is right, Peter. But what's worse is that this circumstance reinforces the Sarah-jealousy from before. It's all a bad set of coincidences."

I began to see Saul's point. This did not look good. I had to trust his instincts in this thing. "What do we do now?"

"Well, I suggest a two-fold approach. They basically have two things on you, Peter. First, there is the 'man scorned' issue. Second, there is the 'man asked to engage in a task he doesn't want to perform' issue. Each can be neutered successfully.

"On the first front you need to find another woman immediately and date her. Have her move in as soon as possible. Get serious. Marry the girl, for heaven's sake."

"Not so easy, Saul."

"Let me finish. So the first thing is to get another woman. The second is to throw yourself wholeheartedly into this Humanity Hospital Case and the Fair Opportunities Initiative in Congress."

"Do I have to?"

"Absolutely. This will show you really cared all along about Moses' work and that the press conference and the other stuff was all a ruse to shake up a fellow traveler."

I winced. I never liked politicians. What Saul was proposing was to do something that was outside from what I really love to do, i.e., read philosophy and think about it, in order to work in the realm of action. I do work in the realm of action in my consulting work, but I get paid handsomely for it.

But working with the court case and Capitol Hill would be *pro bono* only. And *pro bono* doesn't pay the bills. "I don't know, Saul," I began.

Saul took off his glasses again and stared blankly at me. Then he said, "You have to do this, Peter, or we are through. This is it. Find a new woman and throw yourself into this cause."

I saw Saul's point. It was logically correct. However, I was not inclined to follow it. On the other hand, about a third of my consulting income comes directly or indirectly from Saul's firm. I had to comply. "All right. I'll do it. What's the plan?"

"First, I have an appointment with Moses' staff tomorrow at eleven at my office in Balston. I want you to come. You will be a part of the reorganization scheme."

"Reorganization?"

"Yes, step one will be to consolidate our staff. This will mean getting rid of most of the old Common Action people and using my office personnel to take up the slack along with a lobbying firm that I know, Omnium, Ltd."

"Omnium, Ltd.?"

"Yes, they are the ruthless champions of the lobbying—not just in Washington, DC, but all over the world."

I felt suddenly that I was getting out of my depth. Saul sat there staring at me from behind his glasses. "Okay. I'll do it. You'll have to direct me a bit here, I'm afraid."

"Not to worry. Except for a woman named Ulanda Washington, they're all no good. You can feel some satisfaction that Sam Rodriguez will be among the dispossessed."

Saul was right. It did give me some satisfaction. He smiled and gathered his things in order to leave. Then it hit me, "What about the girl, Saul? How am I supposed to get me another woman?"

Saul tilted his head. He hadn't expected this question. But Saul was rarely speechless so he paused and said, "You know Takoma Park?"

"Sure I do," I replied.

"Well, they are having one of their city hall concerts tomorrow afternoon. One of the interns from our office is going. It's supposed to be a great place to meet women who are on the—how should I say, on the impulsive side?" Saul clicked his case shut. "Hey, baby, I can't do EVERYTHING for you. You've got to score that one on your own."

And with that, Saul was gone.

The events of the past days made it impossible for me to read philosophy. Instead, I picked up Moses' journal.

THE JOURNAL OF MOSES LEVI:
JULY 4, 1987

I have decided to resign from my senior partnership in the firm Kovetous and Burling (a major firm in Washington, D.C.). I can no longer live with the fact that I have killed these people.

THE JOURNAL OF MOSES LEVI:
JULY 10, 1987

I have decided to set up a public interest law firm. I have affiliated myself with several environmental and public interest groups. Perhaps I may work out my expiation.

THE JOURNAL OF MOSES LEVI:
JULY 18, 1987

Sarah has brain cancer.

THE JOURNAL OF MOSES LEVI:
JULY 31, 1987

Sarah's brain cancer is progressing rapidly. She is going to die. What am I going to do?

THE JOURNAL OF MOSES LEVI:
SEPTEMBER 21, 1987

Sarah died.

THE JOURNAL OF MOSES LEVI:
OCTOBER 1, 1987

Now it is time for me to incorporate Miriam into my life. I have been such a poor father. Ten years old already. I don't really know her. So many times I meant to do something. Like the time Burning Tree School was going to the Washington Children's Museum. They had been asking for volunteers. Sarah had volunteered, but then couldn't do it. It was my chance. I felt that I had to work that day. I wouldn't have been fired. I was already a partner. An opportunity lost. Now with Sarah gone, so much is lost. What am I going to do?

THE JOURNAL OF MOSES LEVI:
OCTOBER 5, 1987

We can't go on living like this. I never really realized all the things that Sarah had done in my life. Each day. All the little things. Now that she's gone there is such a void that I hardly know how I will cope.

I have to reorganize my life now that I no longer have a job. Fortunately, I was able to pay off the mortgage. With the life insurance and our savings I can actually survive without taking a job, but then what would I do with my time? I need to learn how to live for Miriam, but I feel a responsibility to do more. Somehow I must find a way to do something worthy. But what is worthy?

THE JOURNAL OF MOSES LEVI:
NOVEMBER 10, 1987

I have just finished a month of counseling. My grief support group is wearing thin. This really isn't doing it for me.

THE JOURNAL OF MOSES LEVI:
FEBRUARY 14, 1988

Valentine's Day?

THE JOURNAL OF MOSES LEVI:
FEBRUARY 25, 1988

I have been attending a Reformed Synagogue. So many things that I have never taken the time to do. Miriam goes with me. Perhaps she will take classes for her Bat Mitzvah. I have to be able to do something right.

THE JOURNAL OF MOSES LEVI:
MARCH 1, 1988

I took Miriam to a play at Ford's Theater. Afterwards I took her to a Thai restaurant in Georgetown. I am beginning to form various rituals with my daughter. For example, I am always home to make dinner by 5:30. We discuss school over dinner and then review her studying plan. If she needs help, I try to assist her. I am not the best teacher, but I am determined not to do it for her but to try and teach her how to do it.

When she is ready for bed I read her something and then let her listen to music and read as she goes to sleep. Miriam is a great source of strength. I resolve daily to be a worthy father to her.

CHAPTER NINE

Peter Simon

July 12, 2000

I BEGAN THE DAY very timidly. I drove my car over to campus, parked and took the shuttle bus to Ballston. I didn't know what to expect. We met in Saul's office located in the Ballston area of Arlington. Each of the senior partners in the firm of Cohen, Potts, and Sani headed up an office located in Maryland, the District, and Virginia. Saul's office matched his taste. It was light in color. The walls were all white with hints of tint: very light blue, very light yellow, and very light green. Each hue must have been one position on the color chart away from white itself.

On the walls were pictures of beaches and seascapes. Saul was a beachcomber who loved scavenging various out-of-the-way beaches for assorted shells, driftwood, and miscellaneous junk. Saul would retrieve his gems and make them into lamps, ashtrays, waste cans, and bibelots of all sorts. "What can I say? I love the ocean. It's where we all began," Saul would declare when asked about his menagerie.

The meeting was supposed to be for the remaining skeleton staff of Moses that consisted of four: Sam Rodriguez, Jane Eliot, Ayanna Smith, and Ulanda Washington. From the tone of Saul's message, everyone knew that it was time to clean house.

I was shown into the conference room that consisted of a thin-topped blonde wood table with chrome legs. The chairs were equally delicate and I wondered whether they would fully support my weight. The room was an interior chamber shaped as a large rectangle. On each of the long side walls were curved paintings of the ocean. One showed a storm while the other was pacific.

Seated at the table were Ulanda Washington and Jane Eliot. Rodriguez and Smith had not arrived.

At 11:10, Saul came in with another man who was dressed in a European fitted suit.

"Hello, everyone," began Saul as he sat down. "I would like to begin by introducing you all to Syd Pawalchowski. Syd is going to head this project from here on out."

Syd nodded. He was a tall, thin man with blonde hair. "Syd, this is Ulanda Washington, Jane Eliot, and Peter Simon. I don't know where the other two are. Perhaps they aren't coming."

"Do you want me to call them?" offered Jane.

"No need," said Saul. "This meeting is going to be very short."

"Very short," repeated Syd. Syd spoke with an accent whose origins I could not detect.

"Yes," said Saul turning to Syd. Saul got up and yielded the head of the table to Syd.

"Good morning," said Syd. "I am with you for six months. At the end of that time we will have completed our mission."

"This case started eighteen years ago," said Ulanda. "What makes you think—"

"Our objectives will be precise and we will accomplish them in six months." Ulanda listened with a skeptical look on her face. "I will begin by designating our team. Ms. Washington, you will remain with the team as second in command. Dr. Simon, you will be our public figure. Clerical assistance and legal secretaries will be provided by Mr. Sani's office." Then Syd turned to Jane Eliot, "I am sorry, Ms. Eliot. Your services will not be required. You may return to your employer, Mr. Kaplan."

"Why—I, ah," stammered Jane. She was supposed to be an ally of Moses. All of Moses' staff was. This was a direct affront. It was also a declaration of intelligence. Syd knew that she had been a Kaplan plant.

"You may leave, Ms. Eliot. And tell Ms. Smith and Mr. Rodriguez the same thing. Good day, ma'am."

Jane was visibly shaken. She got up and left. Saul left with her. Now there were just the three of us.

"This will be the core of our team. Ms. Washington will be our lead lawyer. Dr. Simon will be our public figure. And I will be the impresario putting everything together. For the time being, we will meet daily at 8am here in Mr. Sani's conference room. Are there any questions?"

"Thousands of questions," began Ulanda. "To begin, who are you *Mister* Pawalchowski?"

"I am a man behind the scenes. I influence public policy in North America."

"Who do you work for?"

"I work with you to achieve precise goals. We will go over them tomorrow."

"No. But who do you work for, really?"

"I am not a pawn of Common Action, if that is what you mean."

"No. That is not what I mean. Who pays you your salary?"

"I can tell you, but you must keep this part of the operation very secret."

"Why?"

"Trust me. It will not aid our objectives if it comes out."

"I don't like the sound of this. I quit." Ulanda started to get up when Syd reached out and grabbed her arm.

"No. You mustn't. You are critical to the project's success."

"Look whatever-your-name-is-ski, I don't work with people I don't know and I don't work for people I can't trust. Right now you're batting zero for two."

Syd smiled. "You will be a formidable lead lawyer, Ms. Washington. I will tell you whatever you want to know. I normally work for a firm called Omnium, Limited."

"Omnium, Limited? I've never heard of it."

"Not many people have. We like to keep it that way."

"What exactly do you do, Mr. Omnium, Limited?"

"We influence public opinion. We lobby governments. We create favorable climates for our clients so that public policy works in their favor."

"Pretty big job."

"A very big job."

"Must command a very big fee."

Syd chuckled. He was trying to be modest.

"Since this project has almost no money, why have you signed on?"

Syd smiled. "Let's just say that I owe Mr. Sani a favor. This six month stint will repay my debt to him."

"Humph." Ulanda was not fully convinced. "Well, I'll start with you. Who's paying *my* check?"

"Mr. Sani will continue with that."

"Continue?"

"Yes, didn't you know? When Common Action dumped you, Mr. Sani bankrolled the entire operation."

"Damn."

"I'd say so," replied Syd. "Mr. Sani often fools people with his demeanor. He is really a tiger."

Ulanda had no more questions for the moment. Syd turned to me.

"My only question, Syd, is why do we have to meet so early?"

"Actually, 8:00 am is the last time slot I have for this operation each day."

"When's the first?"

"You don't want to know."

He was right about that. And so the meeting was over. Syd vanished, leaving only Ulanda and me.

I was particularly interested to note that Sam Rodriguez didn't bother to show. It would have been so nice if he had. I had imagined everything from a "mano a mano" confrontation to a rather sophisticated recognition that a woman had passed from me to him. No harm done. That's just the way of the world.

Ulanda gave me a piercing look with those baggy brown eyes of hers. "I don't know what to make of that guy."

"Seems like a professional," I replied.

"Yeah, but professional *what*?"

"Don't be so cynical, Ulanda. He seems all right to me."

"Look, Peter, I signed onto this gig because of Moses and *not* because of you."

I gave my hurt look. Ulanda ignored it.

"Fair Opportunity is standing between calm and civil war, baby. I was there when Moses put your face in it. He thought you had some contacts that could do something. He also had some trust in you— though I tell you what, I'm not sure why."

"We were roommates."

"Roommates?"

"At Pembroke."

"That's all?"

"Far as I can see."

"Don't think you got that right. Moses was smarter than that. He could see into things. No. Don't think you got that right."

Maybe I didn't. There were things about Moses I never knew.

THE JOURNAL OF MOSES LEVI:
MARCH 20, 1988

I have thrown myself into Judaism. I don't know why, but it fulfills a very basic need. I am learning Hebrew and absorbing wisdom.

THE JOURNAL OF MOSES LEVI:
JUNE 20, 1988

Miriam is attending a science camp this week. What a wonderful world this has become: to have science camps.

THE JOURNAL OF MOSES LEVI:
JULY 4, 1988

I have volunteered my services to a growing citizens' lobbying group COMMON ACTION. I have thought a lot about Genesis 18:22-33. Sodom is set for destruction because of its iniquity. Abraham and G-d have a chat about how many just people it takes to save a city. I wonder what would have happened if Abraham hadn't stopped at ten? Are the evil redeemed by the one just man? Or are we forced to redeem ourselves?

* * *

I took the Metro over to Takoma Park. Takoma Park is a most interesting city. It used to be split between two counties (Prince George's and

Montgomery) but recently it all came over to Montgomery. The place is out of the 1960s. It is very hip and very liberal. They declared themselves to be a nuclear-free zone during the Cold War. It was a futile gesture since if the U.S. chose to put missile launchers there, they couldn't stop it. If the Soviet Union had chosen to aim a warhead there, they couldn't stop it. It was a futile gesture, but somehow I always felt happiness that they had done it. Perhaps that's why I'm a philosophy professor: I am moved by futile gestures. The city resonated with me in ways that I had long since repressed.

I knew this about Takoma Park long before my visit. I probably would have lived in Takoma Park if I had gotten a job at the University of Maryland or Catholic University. But teaching in Arlington, it would not have been very convenient.

The concert was located at the city hall. It started at two. I was a little early and decided to get a sandwich. I went into a deli that lets you custom order a sandwich for four bucks. It was a great sandwich with pumpernickel bread, sprouts, tomato, chicken slices, and sweet red peppers. I washed it down with a Pennsylvania beer. The place was very busy even though it must have been after the main lunch hour crush.

It was 1:45 when I went into the city hall. The room itself was very functional. It served both for meetings and for concerts such as this. There was also a television camera and sound system to record the event for endless iterations on public access cable television. I sat towards the back. It was not a full house by any means. The crowd seemed to be mainly related to those who were performing.

A group of people would come in and sit together. Then they would cheer loudly when the act began. Finally, after the act they would come up and hug the performers and generally chat it up. No one left early. Many of the acts were folk revival or imitations of various folk, or folk rock (though there was one little boy who played Mozart on the violin). I liked the music, but I was feeling a little tired.

The last act of the afternoon started at four. It was a man and a woman who did Peter, Paul, and Mary songs (minus either Peter or Paul). After a rendition of "Blowin' in the Wind," a woman about thirty sat three chairs away from me on the aisle. There was something about her that was very striking to me. She had blonde hair and seemed to be of average height with very light skin and an intense gaze.

Her concentration on the act allowed me to turn my attention her way without prompting a reciprocal glance. Her eyes were blue and something about her told me she must be intelligent, too.

After the final number of "Leavin' on a Jet Plane," she slid out of her chair and moved to the front. I surmised that she might be the male singer's wife. This seemed evident by the big bear hug she gave him. I am still not sure why I got up and followed her. Perhaps it was my affinity to futile gestures.

"Dave, you were great," I heard her say as I got closer. "I only wish Mom and Dad could have been here."

Mom and dad? This sounded promising.

Dave, who stood about six foot five, merely nodded his head.

"And you were great, too, Holly," she said. "The best husband and wife show on the program."

This cinched it.

Then Holly, who stood much shorter than Dave, said, "Thanks, Andrea. You are very loyal, even though you only came in on our second number. I know you mean it from the bottom of your heart."

"Holly, I've heard most of the other acts before. Remember, there is a lot of repetition in these programs."

Holly took back her reproach with a hug. I decided to step forward.

"I really liked your act. It brought back memories."

Dave shook my hand. Holly nodded her head. Andrea turned and stared at me. "We're all going over to the Rub 'n Stein for a couple of drinks. Do you want to join us?"

I looked to Dave and Holly. They repeated the offer with their facial expressions.

"I'd love to," I said.

And so we went.

CHAPTER TEN

Peter Simon

July 12, 2000

THE FOUR OF US, Dave and Holly along with Andrea and I, went to the Rub 'n Stein. It was set on the order of an English Pub. It was very dark and paneled in Walnut. They served a limited menu of food and an unlimited menu of drinks. Dave took it upon himself to order a pitcher of Heineken.

"When do you get the time to practice?" asked Andrea when the peanuts arrived.

"Well, since we have no kids, it really isn't all that difficult," said Dave.

"I don't have any kids. I'm not even married," began Andrea. "But I don't seem to have time for anything."

"That's because of all those journals you edit," returned Holly. "They keep you busy seven days a week."

Andrea sighed. "Oh, I know. I really should drop one or two, but I'm afraid to do so."

"Why?" asked Holly.

"Well, these trade journals often fold when the economy gets bad. The economy has been so good for so long now that most everyone forgets about what it can be like."

"You mean in a recession like 1990?"

"Exactly. In 1990 I was still in college, but I am told by veterans that about a quarter of the trade journals went under. I met one woman who was editor of the National Association of Grape Growers Journal and the National Association of Mexican American Realtors. Both of them went under in the same year and she had to sell her house. She kept three journals and two thirds of her income disappeared. Presto: almost nothing."

"I couldn't take an existence like that," said Dave.

"That's why you work for the Government," returned his sister.

"Say the 'E.P.A.'"

"The E.P.A."

"That's right. I get *my* paycheck unless the Federal Government shuts down."

"Say the 'E.P.A.,'" returned Andrea.

Dave pretended to swipe at her while Holly shot a mimed gun at her husband.

"He does have it better than either of us, Andrea," said Holly. "You know in my job, I often have to spend hours after the school day on students with particular difficulties."

"Are you a teacher?" I asked Holly.

The three of them suddenly remembered that I was sitting at the table. Holly smiled, "Yes, I am a middle school teacher. I teach autistic children."

"What a challenge," I said.

"Somebody has to be there for them," said Holly. As she spoke, I realized that she had a very broad face. I tried to imagine what it would be like being under her care. She was a zealot for good.

"Not just *somebody*," I replied. "'Somebody' generally means 'somebody else.' You've taken the responsibility upon yourself. I know. I mean I don't know. But I can guess. You see I'm a teacher, too. So I can imagine by analogy what you are going through."

"Oh really, you're a teacher?" Andrea asked. "Where do you teach?"

"I teach at Notre Dame-Loyola in Arlington, Virginia."

"Isn't that a girls' college?"

"It used to be, but now it's a coed, comprehensive university— meaning that they give a number of master's degrees and post-masters certificates."

"So you're a college professor," said Holly.

"I'm a teacher, or at least I try to be. But when I come into contact with someone who has to be so good at what she does as to be able to reach autistic children, I'm in total awe. I admire people like you."

Holly's fortress opened and she smiled. "Thank you. Did you have an autistic child in your past?"

"Yes and no. Not personally, but I was married once, now divorced, and my wife, Julia, used to baby-sit for one of the top Milton scholars in the world. She had an autistic child. Julia used to tell me about it."

"So you're a single college professor teaching at Notre Dame-Loyola?" continued Holly.

"Yes, I'm a philosopher."

"A philosopher?" replied Andrea. "I took two classes in philosophy when I was in college."

"Oh really? Where did you go to college?"

"Brown. I graduated in '94. English major."

"English? I've always liked literature. My first book was on integrating Hegel's ethics, my dissertation, into a theory of English Criticism."

Then the beer came.

* * *

When we had finished, Dave and Holly said goodbye leaving, Andrea and me in front of the pub. We watched the pair depart, and then Andrea turned to me and said, "Do you like the WNBA?"

"What's the WNBA?" I replied.

"Do you want to go somewhere with me?"

"Sure," I said.

"Let's get to the Metro."

It seems that the WNBA is the Women's National Basketball League that in Washington is a gathering place for women who want to reaffirm their commitment toward the cause. I had no problem with this so long as there was room for me in the mosaic. We took the Metro to Chinatown and got some real food at a place just next to the big red pagoda gate. The meal was good, and it was cheap. We split the bill.

Then we walked a couple of blocks to the MCI Center and a professional basketball game. I used to love basketball, but after college hadn't dribbled a ball nor even watched the game on television. It was as if something long forgotten was being re-awakened. It was the sort of feeling that I used to have with Sarah Z.

Andrea was a take-charge woman. I liked that. It took such a burden from me.

Andrea bought the tickets (I had virtually run out of cash, so the game was on her). We sat at midcourt, two rows up from the first general walkway. They were great seats. I must say that I really enjoyed the game. The emphasis upon good fundamental play reminded me of when I learned the game. It was refreshing.

*   *   *

We parted our ways at Metro Center. Andrea and I were headed toward different directions. We exchanged phone numbers and vague commitments to call.

As I rode back to Ballston I thought about Andrea. She was certainly different from Monique. Monique used to advertise the fact that she was a painter to extort a rather ridiculously one-sided set of rules. *She* could come and stay with me at my house as long as it suited her, but whenever she had something better to do, she would tell me that she wouldn't be back for a week or two (sometimes a month or two). It was rather disconcerting. However, if *I* was ever not totally available to her whenever she wanted me, there was hell to pay.

Why did I put up with it? I don't know. I have always been a survivor. When things don't turn my way I try to adapt. Monique put adaptation to the ultimate test. It wasn't as if she was all that good-looking or very accommodating in bed, either. Monique was haughty. In the academic world we are taught that haughty equals high quality. I suppose that I fell for Monique and put up with her because she was haughty.

I really don't know. I have never been very good with women. When I taught at Marquette I met and married Julia. Julia taught English literature. She went in for all the newfangled literary theories such as Deconstructionism. Julia fell in love with Deconstructionism. She applied it to our marriage. After finding a contradiction that couldn't be resolved, she ended it.

Andrea wasn't like either Julia or Monique, but she did remind me of Sarah Z. I don't know what it is, but there is a sort of sincerity of purpose that makes me think of Sarah.

I also thought that what Andrea might be looking for is a form of stability that might enable her to jettison a journal or two and not be afraid of an economic downturn. She is a woman living and working on the edge. I am a man living in emptiness, without purpose. Albert Camus once said that the ultimate philosophical question is why we don't commit suicide. It is a question that we must ask every day. It is also a loaded question. It is loaded because it implies other questions, as well. If I say, "I choose not to kill myself today," it is because there is a *reason* not to kill myself today. That reason is a purpose. A purpose is something like an "end" or *telos*. When I authentically decide not to kill myself it is because I have created a purpose for living. This purpose is the essence of life. It conveys meaning to everything else.

When you live in emptiness, you live without purpose. When you live without purpose, it is only accidental that you don't suddenly kill yourself.

THE JOURNAL OF MOSES LEVI:
8/8/88

What a wonderful date. Miriam and I along with a family from our synagogue are on vacation in Maine. I wish I had found the time for family vacations when Sarah was alive. We miss so much in our striving for whatever it is that we call our life. In my case, it was just a buzz and a swirl without much regard for direction.

THE JOURNAL OF MOSES LEVI:
OCTOBER 25, 1988

Miriam and I heard about a wonderful farm that lets you pick your own pumpkin. It's only a half-hour away—up county. It was a nice day and when we got home we carved one of the craziest pumpkins ever. I volunteered to take a group of neighborhood kids around on Halloween.

THE JOURNAL OF MOSES LEVI:
APRIL 7, 1989

I took Miriam to the opening day of the Baltimore Orioles. It's been so long since I've been to a baseball game. Miriam likes baseball in school so I thought it would be a nice day out. There is something about the pace of a baseball game that is so much more civilized than the pace that I used to live my life.

THE JOURNAL OF MOSES LEVI:
APRIL 19,1990

Miriam and I went on a House Building Weekend with Habitat for Humanity in S.E. D.C. I am not much of a carpenter, but I could do the go-for work and assist with many unskilled tasks. I think that Miriam enjoyed herself, too.

We live in such a land of contrasts: rich and poor, black and white, advantaged and disadvantaged. The distribution of such things is clearly an instance of injustice. When any man of good faith witnesses injustice, he must act.

CHAPTER ELEVEN

Josh Kaplan, Director of Common Action

July 5, 1996

"**LADIES AND GENTLEMEN.** We are at a crossroads. In the space of the six years since I was hired at Common Action as an attorney right out of Marquette University Law School, I have tried to bring to my job the kind of Midwestern sensibility that I thought the task needed. After all, things work *differently* here on the East Coast." The crowd tittered a bit. I expected them to. Then I turned the page and found that my notes were totally out of order! Instantly, I decided that I had two options: to search for the right page and look like a fool or to *ad lib* and look like a fool. What a choice.

I stepped away from the podium to let them know that I was speaking from the heart. "There have been many battles. We began as a shoestring operation that depended upon most of its workers being volunteer. But we stayed true to our charge to be a balancing force in the political climate of Washington. We seek to counteract the special interest lobbyists by being a lobbyist for the People of the United States of America." The last words were given special emphasis. Always a good move. Everyone likes to applaud the name of their country—especially those liberals who fancy themselves to be supporters of Common Action.

"As your new Director, I seek to move the action group in directions that will continue to expand our mission as a gadfly to the powered and rich. We will fight for environmental reform, equal opportunity for all, and the rights of the ordinary citizen because it is the ordinary citizen that is the backbone of this great nation of ours." Another applause line, but it was flatter than expected.

"I now set out a new challenge for our organization. This will be the theme of my administration. My challenge to you is to return to our origins. Though we have been very successful during the last three years in fundraising, I suggest to you that our future depends upon our enlisting an army of volunteers who will spread across this country of ours enlisting our theme of the need for political participation in our democracy. That's right, political participation by all Americans, whether they agree with us or not. This must become our common vision.

"It is only when America comes together with that same spirit of self-governance that we can bring power back to the people." I decided to hit my fist with my open left hand so that it made a smacking sound. Very forceful. I had their attention.

"Our present path will lead to government by the rich—plutocracy, I think they call it. This will eventually devolve into tyranny. We have something better. We have democracy—the rule by the people, *all* of the people. Common Action will focus its energy toward fulfilling its aim: empowering common action. I think that we can be on the vanguard of a period of national renewal.

"As your new Director, I am thankful for the opportunity to be the one to lead you there. Let us go forward and bring back government to the people and restore democracy to our great country. Thank you."

Pretty good applause. Might have been better, but it was a solid response. Nothing to jeopardize our baseline. I have decided to restructure our organization. In the past we have been an undisciplined group of various pet projects. Each project got a manager and he or she set about to get funding after some meager seed money. This meant that we really had many different directions that we pursued. Each project was a mini-agency with the project manager as the head. This has to stop.

I sat in my seat as Rosmarie brought the meeting to a conclusion. Then there was the reception. Two goals: new direction and more funding.

--yes, thank you. I'm glad you liked it.

--oh not really, I was always very happy for the six years I worked on other people's projects and then to my own.

--yes, thank you. I'm glad you liked it.

--I was never in favor of that project either. I think we need to create a system of more centralized authority. But you know every new agenda requires funding!

--I'm glad you liked it. I think the future looks awfully good for us, but we will never get there without more funding.

--More funding is essential.

--we can't make it happen without more money. We work at a fraction of the budget that the fat cats throw out. You've got to remember, money talks.

--money talks.

--more funding

more money money money money money money money

* * *

So many of the backers of Common Action are such arrogant assholes. Champagne Socialists! Let's share around--so long as it does not cut into my champagne budget! I'm from Milwaukee. I'm a beer man. Let them eat pretzels!

I held my first staff meeting the next week. We occupy the fourth floor of a renovated house that is off Dupont Circle just adjacent to Connecticut Avenue. The nicest space in the joint is our conference room. It is here that we bring contributors and supporters so that they might get a sense of our mission. There is a multi-media system including slides, movies, video, and a new Internet projection system (that I pushed for).

Three of our five senior project coordinators were on time. Then Ulanda Washington showed up (she's always late). The only absent body was Moses Levi. This guy is the most talented person in our organization, but definitely a loose cannon. You can never predict what he will say. The guy marches to the beat of a different drummer.

This has been the problem with this organization, if you want to know the truth. We have let ourselves become a loose confederation of individuals each doing his or her own thing. This is fine for those individuals who are looking for a way to further their own personal self-expression, but it does not do much for the organization itself.

I decided to start the meeting.

"Good afternoon. I wanted this meeting to reflect some of the changes that we will undergo now that I am the Director of Common Action. We all know each other, but we do not know each other through our new roles. This is important. I feel that there is always an opportunity for renewal each time an organization changes leadership. What I want to do with you is to outline the direction I believe in and how we will transition towards that direction."

"Come on, Josh. What is this crap?" said Margo. Margo is the oldest of our senior project coordinators. She is also the most vocal.

"Hear me out, Margo. I've gotten approval from our Board for everything that I'm going to tell you this afternoon."

Margo screwed up her face and started playing with her kinky hair that was often uncombed.

"As I was saying," I began again. "Things are going to change around here."

"Why?" asked Ulanda.

"Let's hold your skepticism until I'm done." Ulanda nodded her head.

"In our present system we have a system that allows each of you to pick and choose your projects subject to approval of this committee and the Director. The result has been a hodgepodge of different projects all going in their own direction. Often they go in contradictory directions!" I looked up from my prepared comments to see what response I was getting. Maria, Kristen, and Ulanda were stone faced. Margo was still working with her hair.

"What I propose is that we create a more unified image to the world. We will stand for participatory democracy. This will be our mission. All other projects will have to revolve around that central mission. The mission will focus us towards both projects and how we will implement them.

"Senior project coordinators will become divisional heads each concentrating upon a region of the country and handling all issues within that region. This will include *all* projects in that region as well as *all* fundraising activities."

"You're making us into fundraisers?" asked Kristen Engman, our token statuesque Nordic beauty.

"I'm empowering you to do everything you want to. From soup to nuts you will now be in charge of *everything*." Just as I uttered the phrase, 'you will now be in charge of everything,' Moses Levi walked in. He was talking on his cell phone that was positioned between his shoulder and his jaw and he was manipulating a calculator in one hand while swinging his famous black leather bag in the other. That bag (everyone says) must be a hundred years old. It was probably very high quality when it was made way back when, but now it is a relic of another age. I'm not into relics. I'm going to change the world.

Moses got off his phone, plopped down next to Ulanda, opened his case so that he could deposit his calculator and with the same motion brought out a liverwurst sandwich. I mean really, who eats liverwurst sandwiches who is under a hundred years old? He unwrapped the stained brown paper and took a large bite that he chewed with relish. When he had swallowed that bite, he lay down his sandwich onto that greasy brown piece of paper and looked around to all of us. "Sorry I'm late. I was visiting a couple of guys, you know—Dalton Smith and Maurice Jones. They're up for murder in Northern Virginia. It looks like all their appeals for commuting their death penalty sentence are at the end." Moses took another bite of his grotesque sandwich.

"It ran over. I'm sorry. I've got to file a writ on their behalf this afternoon so I'll have to cut out early if this is going to be a long meeting." Moses spoke to all the others but he did not look at me. I am sitting at the head of the table, and I am the Director of this organization. I could have his ass if I chose for such rudeness.

"No, Moses, it won't be long. I'm just going over our re-organization plans."

"He's making us fundraisers," bitched Kristen.

"Yeah, and assigning us to regions of the country," put Ulanda.

"What he's doing is to create a new more highly centralized organization that is designed to more effectively get across his signature message of participation in democracy through decentralization and citizen involvement," said Maria Lugones. I never really liked Maria. She went to Santa Clara where they don't give any grades: kind of a loosey goosey kind of place. I believe in what Will Rogers said, "Shake the country and everything loose falls to California." Thinks her general studies degree from Santa Clara is better than my History degree from

Marquette! And just because she worked as a paralegal once, she's all of a sudden an expert on the law.

"Did I hear you correctly?" asked Moses (his mouth full of his third bite of sandwich). "We're going to centralize to promote decentralization?"

"Bingo," snapped Margo.

Moses started to gag. Kristen gave him her Evian bottle. After that little scene I felt it was necessary to take charge.

"You all have the new agenda on your e-mail. I copied all of you. I'm not here to debate its merits. It is a *fait accomplis.* I've already cleared it with the Board."

"You went forward to the Board without consulting us?" asked Moses.

"What? Am I the only one in this room with a head on his shoulders? H-e-l-l-oooo. I am after all the executive Director of Common Action. I am only responsible to the Board. I do have the authority to fire and hire." I looked around at each of them. When I got to Moses, he was handing me the last three bites of his blasted sandwich.

"Do you want my resignation?"

"Resignation? It looks like a greasy sandwich that is dripping all over the new conference table that I just bought."

"Do you want my resignation?" he repeated.

"What is this? Mass revolt?"

"You have every *right* to do everything you've done, Josh," began Maria. "No one is objecting to that. We couldn't sue you under our non-profit Directors and Officers Insurance Liability policy. You are within your legal domain."

I nodded. I never thought I'd get Maria on my side. Of all the seniors save for Moses, I thought she'd be my hardest case. I broke into a smile.

"What you don't understand, Josh, is that the worldview under which we work is so totally different from the vision that you're presenting to us. We don't want the most efficient organization possible. We're after our own personal missions to do good. For whatever our reasons, we work just above the poverty line because we feel called to it. If you fail to grasp this fact then I'm with Moses, count me out."

"Me too," came the response of the other three almost instantly.

"What is this?" I said. "A mutiny?"

"Yes," replied Kristen. "And *you*, Josh, are the mutineer."

I got up and started pacing. "I don't think any of you are tuned in to our present situation. Sure we've grown the past few years, but our net equity is very poor. We're on the brink of going out of business in a climate of unprecedented economic growth. Charities left and right are building up their endowments. Endowments. Do you know what our endowment is? I'll tell you: twelve fucking million dollars. Do you know how far twelve million dollars will get an organization that has an annual budget of 80 million dollars?" I moved to the table and slammed down both hands. "To the fuckin poor house and non-existence, that's what. Do you know that the Ford Foundation pays for 95% of its annual expenses from its endowment? Rockefeller is 87%. Do you know what we can pay? Five percent of twelve million is six hundred thousand dollars. Can you believe that? A non-profit today is *not* taken seriously unless it has an endowment that covers at least 50% of its operating costs. You cannot be so dependent upon yearly contributions or else you will perish."

I got up and walked over to the new Deer Park water cooler I had installed in our conference room. I got out a recyclable paper cup, poured it to the rim and then drained it. "You all are so all high and mighty about your commitment to your projects. Well, fuck your projects. If there isn't money there, then there are no projects."

While I was talking I noted that Moses was methodically finishing his lunch. He took out a handkerchief and cleaned his fingers and lips of the disgusting grease. When I had finished he said, "Josh. Tell me this. Would you have a problem with implementing your grand design in stages?" Moses looked to the others and they were nodding.

What was I to say? I already had them. It was only a matter of time. "What do you mean, Moses?"

"What I'm thinking of is this. We all get together and take it as a given that at time X, this organization, will be exactly as you describe it. But as a cooperative unit we will determine together just how we get there. After all, if we move too precipitously all at once, then we are liable to alienate just those contributors that could make our endowment the envy of other non-profits."

I didn't know how to take Moses. He's a very difficult cat.

"So what do you say, Josh? Shall we work on a transition plan together—one that each of us at this table can live with, or do you want to simply clean house and create your own fiefdom?"

I paused. My own fiefdom would be nice. But I caught his drift. If I let these people go, then they'd start another non-profit on their own and in no time would have more total assets than Common Action. This was no choice. This was an ultimatum from one who held the upper hand. I had to cave. But what I still *could* do was to work at getting rid of my arch enemy, Moses Levi.

I smiled and offered my hand to Moses. "Perhaps I've been too brash in my youthful enthusiasm. Of course you're right. Consensus is the proper path. We'll work out a transition plan together."

CHAPTER TWELVE

Peter Simon

July 13, 2000

8:00 ANTE MERIDIAN. I made it on time. This was no small feat because I had left my car all night at Notre Dame-Loyola. Not on purpose, of course. But when I got back from the basketball game to the Ballston Metro stop, it was 11:15 p.m. This meant that since the college shuttle stops running at eleven, I had to hoof it home (a distance of two miles, if you know how to do it). This had given me time to think.

I decided to repeat the trek in the morning since it was a three-mile walk to campus and since there is very poor parking at Ballston. I judged that a two-mile walk would take me around forty minutes. I was there in thirty-eight.

When I arrived, I met Saul. "Peter, how are you?"

Most of the staff had already arrived. "You all start early around here, don't you?"

Saul put his arm around my shoulder. His graying hair on the sides of his bald head seemed to shine. "Oh, don't worry about them. We have three shifts around here, that way we're covered from 7:00 to 7:00."

"I'm impressed. Every time I've done something for you I've been here around noon."

"That's your time of the day, baby. That's when you start cooking." When Saul talked he seemed to have so much enthusiasm that it sometimes worried me. Does this guy ever have a 'slow' speed?

"Is Syd here yet?"

"Syd? You mean the 'Duke of Omnium'?"

"The Duke of Omnium?" I repeated.

"That's what they call him. He's so important and can do so much that his moniker is The Duke of Omnium."

I pondered this situation for a moment. I was dealing not only with a shadow man who the world barely knew, but they called him The Duke of Omnium. A duke is the highest person in the medieval fiefdom, save the king. This man must be the controller of everything!

Ulanda was already there going over some points with the Duke. I sat down and opened a two-inch bound document that had been prepared for me. On the first piece of the book was the heading: Project Goals.

PROJECT GOALS

I.   Humanity Hospital Case

   A.   Use Inside Leverage to settle the appeal quickly

   B.   Create the proper background response for our eventual loss

II.   Fair Opportunity Initiative

   A.   Contact Senator Blight in order to force a losing bill to a vote

   B.   Create the proper background response to further the work of the new action committee.

III. Create Fair Opportunity Action Committee

   A.   Find a Host Organization

   B.   Work at creating infrastructure

IV.   Work on Public Relations

   A.   Create a set of "talking points"

   B.   Create a strategy to implement the talking points into the national media

   C.   Work with Peter Simon so that he becomes a suitable spokesman for the Cause.

Obviously, I was most drawn to point IV. This seemed to have the most to do with me. The Duke had said that I was to be the spokesman for the group. This meant that I would supplant a place that Moses had once filled.

Moses during the last nine months had been on the nightly news, and in February the major newsmagazines. He carried himself well in those venues. His litigation skills proved valuable. Of course, what got to me were Moses' tricks (particularly when they were directed against *me*). For example, he contacted me about doing a press conference with him on Fair Opportunity. He told me he was just enlisting allies who believe in opportunity for all. Who could object to that?

So I went and got sandbagged when he calls on me to join him—not just in moral support—but in actually signing onto the project giving my non-existent time and vague, unknown resources to the project. I mean, this was a press conference that was covered by all the major networks and CNN. And what does Moses do? He turns his magic wand into a snake to bite me.

"And now, Peter, I invite you to put your deeds into the lofty words you've just expressed and to join the Common Action Fair Opportunity Initiative as a leading spokesman, bringing your keen intelligence and the considerable clout of your consulting clients behind you!" There were cheers from the claques. All the cameras were turned on *me*. What was I to say? If I say 'yes,' then he has me at his beck and call. This asshole who stole my fiancée while I was studying abroad. This opportunist who dropped philosophy for the law when he realized how much money he could make there. Then he makes his money, feels a little dirty, and turns his life over to good works. Bullshit.

Of course, some of this I didn't know at the time. It has only been since I began reading his diary that I learned about the *other* Moses. Still, I thought it was a cheap trick to put me on the spot like that. As you can see, 'yes' was not an option appealing to me.

If I say 'no,' then I look like a hypocrite who espouses one thing and does another. This stance could hurt me considerably with my consulting clientele. These law firms and businesses hire me to talk to them about business ethics. The underlying supposition is that I am a man who has followed his convictions in life to become a teacher (despite the low remuneration) because I believed in doing what I knew was right. It is quite a nice little platform to part rich-conflicted-bastards from their wallets. Most of these people (I have just as many female as male clients these days) are decent folk who have done what it takes within their field to win. However, as they get older, they realize that winning has its price. That's where I come in. I castigate them and make them feel bad about what they have done and prompt them to take a vow to reform. It is, perhaps, only a few steps removed from sadomasochistic prostitutes who tie their clients up and then whip them.

At any rate, the whole enterprise depends upon these clients of mine viewing me as a man of my word and a non-hypocrite. Thus 'no' is not an option.

When both 'yes' and 'no' are not options, then the agent (me) is forced into what is called a dilemma situation. A dilemma situation occurs when one is forced to choose between two unacceptable alternatives. Thus, I baked for an eternity of several seconds as I considered my options as national television captured my every indecisive weakness.

"Certainly, I'll help you, Moses. But you know I'm just a lowly philosopher. Rather a neophyte in the powerful realm in which you navigate."

Moses only smiled and embraced me. I smiled. He smiled. And I'm sure half of the country smiled at this farce.

*   *   *

Later there were the details. Moses had invited me to a luncheon at the legendary Papa Giovanni's Restaurant just off Dupont Circle. It was there that Moses bombarded me with detailed information about my life and my consulting clients. Moses knew it all. He became very pushy. He wanted me to deliver Cohen, Potts, and Sani to make up for (what I now know) was the almost total loss of financial support from Common Action. Their leader, Josh Kaplan, has an ego the size of Jupiter. He could not run an organization in which there was another who might eclipse him. He was pushing Moses out.

Moses needed to keep things going. He was a desperate man. Somehow he discovered various items of information about me. Did he employ a private detective service? Or did he do the dirty work himself? I guess I'll never know now that he seems to have disappeared. Perhaps he killed himself? Perhaps he just dropped out like so many of the counter cultural figures of the 60s and 70s when mainstream America became so unbearable to them. I don't know.

What I do know is that when he got on my case about helping him in just the way he wanted, it brought back voices from the past—voices that I had long thought were dead. They weren't. They were only sleeping. Now they were awakened and they stirred my emotional *thymos* to such an extent that I could not control myself. I just had to shut him up.

So, over our main course of gourmet cuisine I punched him squarely in the nose. It was only the second time that I had ever hit Moses. Then the magic occurred again. Instantly there were people in the restaurant with cameras. (You have to understand that Papa Giovanni's is a very small restaurant with only five or six tables.) Moses must have had plants. He had staged the entire thing. I was under his almighty power.

This also made the national press. MOSES LEVI ATTACKED BY NEW SPOKESMAN! They say that all publicity is good publicity. That may have been true in Moses' case, but not in mine.

I don't know what came over me. It was as if we were transported to Pembroke and I had discovered that he had stolen Sarah Z. from me. It was the same Moses who had never appreciated all I had done to help *him* not flunk out of Pembroke. Such ingratitude. Stealing my girl. There's such a thing as loyalty.

I'm sorry that I hit Moses. I am a man of the mind and not of the brawn. But I know that given the circumstances played over again, I'd have done the same.

I wonder if Moses knew that. Sometimes I think the guy is an agent of God (except that I don't believe in God). At any rate, he can be prescient. And he was damn lucky. So now I am willingly taking on the job that he wanted me to take but I had refused. Moses wins again.

Saul had told me that what I needed to do in order to get out of the grasp of Alice Minkas and her minion, Henry Hoover, was to undercut their two best arguments by throwing myself into Fair Opportunity Initiative and by flitting to another woman.

I am not, by nature, inclined to choose whatever is in my best interest as a directive of action. My personal history is a testament that I often—if not habitually—act contrary to my self-interest. Thus, Saul's advice really ran against the grain with me. The prime mitigating factor is that I really support the intellectual basis of the Fair Opportunity Initiative. It seems correct to me. I believe that those who are against Affirmative Action make their case upon two premises: 1) Affirmative Action is a group solution to a phenomenon that is individual in its nature. Because of this logical mistake, it is a flawed policy. 2) Affirmative Action undercuts the notion of fair rewards: desert. We all believe in fair rewards ergo, Affirmative Action is unjust.

Each of these refutations is challenging in its own way. But both refutations are flawed. In the first case it *is* true that discrimination occurs on the individual level. Mr. X discriminates against Mr. Y. As a result of this act, Y has a claim to redress against X in virtue of the rule of law that has at its very minimum the principle of treating like cases similarly.

A group solution lumps those who *have not* discriminated in the same logical class as those who *have*. In this way it might be said that those who are improperly classified have been treated unfairly.

In a pure sense, this refutation is true. The problem is that the dynamics of Affirmative Action constitute a case of comparative disadvantage. That is, it may be wrong to put some good non-discriminating folk into a class that yokes them with the perpetrators of the discrimination, but it does less harm than failing to put forth a solution to redress the victims of discrimination. This is particularly evident when one examines the second case of deserts.

In deserts theory it is often said that one deserves the functional outcome of his own work. This is a good definition, but it begs the question of what constitutes one's own work. Take the case of two puzzle makers. Each is given a difficult 1,000 piece puzzle to complete in a given time interval. Puzzle maker A is presented a puzzle already 80% complete. Puzzle maker B is presented a puzzle with a few random pieces set together—no more than 5%. Then we ask each to complete the puzzle. Let us say that puzzle maker A finishes his task and puzzle maker B only gets 65% of the way through. The question is who deserves to be rewarded as 'Best Puzzle Maker'?

Some would say that the title belongs to A because only he completed the puzzle. Others would demur because A was given an almost completed puzzle. The difficulty involved with working out the early stages of puzzle making is so much more complex than the later stages that it is difficult to compare. If the time interval had been extended, then surely B would have completed his puzzle as well. But there is only so much time allotted in life. The fact that B did so much in the time allotted to him is significant. He completed over 3 times the amount that A did. Even if we imagine a third contestant, C, who started with nothing and completed only 25%, he would have done more than A had.

This is not to say that if A had been put in the position of B or C that he, too, might have matched their results. We don't know. We'll never know. That is the point.

What we do know is that A had it a lot easier than B or C. A's actual accomplishment is less than B or C. If one is rewarded according to how much of the puzzle he completes, then actually B and C *deserve* more than A does. But as we all know, society does not *really* reward upon deserts. They reward on how much of the puzzle lies completed before you. This is not fair.

Affirmative Action is one strategy to rectify this unfairness. It seeks an imperfect means to allow an extra credit to be given to those of equal capability much as a veteran's preference has been given in the past to those who have served in the armed forces.

The discontent do not see it in this way. They view the extra credit as undeserved. After all, they say, why does being a victim entitle you to anything—unless we were the ones who did it to you?

However, this ignores the systemic difficulties that emerge when numbers of people act prejudicially against others. The only practical means of creating a system of redress is through a policy of the state.

Moses' genius was to observe that Affirmative Action has worked with a certain group of once disadvantaged people such that some individuals within the disadvantaged group are no longer disadvantaged. This means (for example) that some African American individuals are now advantaged, and though African Americans are, as a group, disadvantaged, there are some individuals that are now advantaged. (The same holds true for other disadvantaged groups such as Latinos and Native Americans.) The flip side to this is that there are some disadvantaged individuals from advantaged groups (such as Caucasians of Western European Descent and Asians from China, Korea, and Japan).

Thus, what Moses did was to recognize that at the edges things had changed and so the policy needed to be changed. Instead of junking Affirmative Action, he advocated keeping it for the bulk in the middle. At the edges, the top and bottom 20%, there would be a change. African American families who had made it and were making hefty six figure salaries no longer needed the help of Affirmative Action. On the same token, white and Asian families who were in the bottom 20% should be brought into the net of Fair Opportunity.

This change in policy to include economic origins is meant to go back to the puzzle maker case. Those in society who are wealthy are like the puzzle maker who has 80% completed. They do not deserve any more help even though they may be subject to individual discrimination. Their starting place advantage exempts them from societal assistance.

Those in society who are poor are disadvantaged, whatever their ethnicity.

I support these ideas. Therefore, intellectually, I felt prepared to become Moses' surrogate.

As to the second of Saul's recommendations, viz., flitting to another woman, I now need no soul-searching discussions. In fact, I had an appointment with Andrea to attend a lecture at Georgetown on Thomas Hardy at 5:30 to be followed by dinner and discussion. This was very much to my liking.

CHAPTER THIRTEEN

Peter Simon

July 13, 2000

AFTER THE LECTURE, Andrea and I went to a little Italian restaurant just over M Street toward the river. Neither of us had driven to Georgetown. I had taken a bus from Ballston and walked the rest of the way, while Andrea had taken the Metro to Dupont Circle and caught a bus from there. (There is no Metro stop in Georgetown. Can't mix with the hoi polloi and all that, I suppose.) The lecture, which was in Gaston Hall, was very interesting. About eighty people showed up. The speaker, Agatha Crispen, has a world class reputation in the 19th Century British Novel. She set forth the thesis that Hardy (protestations to the contrary) really did believe in a god, but that the god was a trickster. The good were often punished and the evil were sometimes exalted. This was a sort of Job-like point to test the resolve of humankind. Thus, in novels like *Jude the Obscure* or *The Trumpet Major* or any of the mid-to-late works, it is clear that "virtue rewarded" is not the agenda of the day.

The lecture stimulated our conversation as we sat down in the dimly lit bistro that is a haunt for Georgetown students. We were lucky enough to sit near a window and could pretend that the several students around us didn't exist. (Think how much worse it would have been if school were in regular session!)

The restaurant is rather dark. The ceiling is vaulted with rough wooden beams doing the necessary labor. Attached to the beams is fish netting that loops up and down from the ceiling with colored glass balls attached to the netting. I suppose they are supposed to be floating balls that hold up the net once it's thrown into the water?

The ball motif is repeated again on the tables as a candleholder. A conic section of the ball is removed so that the candle may shine forth. The irregularities in the glass create a rather pleasant refraction of colors.

The tables are wooden with beige linen place mats. The presence of so much wood gives the place warmth.

I looked at Andrea sitting across from me. One side of her face was in the light from the window while the other was in a gray shadow. It was 7:30 p.m. and the day was dissolving away.

"I can almost see the canal," said Andrea.

She was talking about the C & O canal. This canal (now only a tourist attraction) was begun in the early 1800s as a way to connect little Washington, DC with points north and west. In its time, it would have been a technological advancement that could have brought thousands to its investors. However, the railroad emerged before the canal was completed and it could do everything the canal could do (and more) in half the time. Instant obsolescence. This is the reason one does not devote his soul to technology!

"Yes," I replied. "It's rather obscure, but it's there."

Andrea laughed.

It is nice to talk to someone who understands language. Sarah Z. used to be like that. Andrea looked nothing like Sarah (almost the opposite, in fact), but something about Andrea reminded me of Sarah.

"But tell me," she said. "Do you agree with the speaker at the lecture that God is a trickster?"

"I don't believe in God," I replied.

"That has nothing to do with my question," said Andrea.

"Ah, a literary foray. I see. Given the worldview of Hardy, I'd say that I could agree."

"Remember," said Andrea, pointing her finger at me. "Hardy was an atheist, too."

"Then what's the point?"

"Hardy was an atheist who was consumed with thinking about God. What was Hardy thinking about?" The waiter came by with three pieces of freshly cooked bread that presented a wonderful yeasty aroma to our table.

I took my eyes off the bread and looked back to Andrea. "A thought. A speech act. A linguistic convention. There are various turns to this, you know."

"But none of them turn to God?"

"So you are a nominalist?" I queried.

"I'm not sure what you mean. But when I was an undergraduate at Pembroke—"

"—Pembroke? I thought you attended Brown. Class of '94."

"Oh, that was my master's degree. My bachelor's degree is from Pembroke, class of '92. I guess that makes me a little older than you thought."

"Yeah, as if age would make a difference to a man like me."

"What sort of man are you?" It was time for me to grab a piece of bread. It was still warm to the touch. I held the bread in my hand like a prop.

"A Pembroke graduate, class of '74," I said, gesturing with my prop.

"Oh really. You went to Pembroke?"

"Oh certainly I did. Back in the old days. Before they closed the tunnels."

"They had to do that, you know. Safety."

"Bullshit." I started after my bread. I didn't want it to go cold. "On that same argument they should close the Arboretum because you never know who might be lurking behind a tree somewhere. There is the doctrine of implied consent to risk. If you go to a baseball game there is the possibility that a foul ball will hit you in the head and kill you. It is a risk you knowingly take each time you buy a baseball ticket."

"Well, I'm glad I don't care for baseball," replied Andrea.

"Me neither. I just wanted to make the point. If someone is afraid of being attacked, then do not go into the tunnels."

"But they are an enticing risk, as they say. You know, if you build a swimming pool and even construct the mandatory six-foot fence around it, and a youngster climbs over the fence and drowns, you can still be liable because a swimming pool is enticing. In the same way, heating tunnels below forty-degree below zero outside temperatures could be considered to be enticing."

"I suppose you have a point," I conceded. "But all the same, it was very nice for me when I went to Pembroke. You ran into the most interesting people down there." I sighed wistfully and took a drink of water.

"So getting back to my original question, was the speaker right about the nature of God?" Andrea was nothing if she wasn't persistent.

"I don't know. I must confess that I do not spend too much time thinking about that which I don't believe exists."

"Maybe it's the name that has you befuddled. Have you ever read Thomas Aquinas?" She lifted her glass of water and took another sip.

"Not really. Medieval philosophy is too dedicated to God, and since I don't believe in God. . ." Andrea smiled at my comment and leaned forward.

"Aquinas concentrated upon the properties of God and not the name, itself. This is also a strategy adopted by the Jews and Muslims."

"What are you, a priest or something?"

"No. Religion was my minor at Pembroke," said Andrea, leaning back.

"So what's your point?"

"My point is first that you need not believe in a conventional idea of God to entertain my question. All you need to do is accept fundamental notions of finality."

"Teleology?"

"That's right. Second, you have to wonder whether the end is always the good of the process or whether it may sometimes be a false appearance meant to trick you." Andrea took a long drink of her water— just about finishing the glass.

"I have trouble with the word, 'meant.' For an atheist, that is a loaded word."

"Yes it is. But so is 'purpose' and 'end.' I think that Hardy— whether he knew it or not—was accepting the fundamental sense of God that Aquinas talked about. The letters: g-o-d are irrelevant since what I am talking about can have no name. This is because naming something limits it and what I'm talking about has no limits."

"So how do you talk about this—whatever—if you can't name it? Isn't naming an essential process in the philosophy of denoting and rigid designation?" Andrea stopped and pursed her lips. Then she reached out for a slice of the bread. She took the time to butter her piece. She was in no hurry.

"You've got me with that jargon. I'm not a philosopher. I'm not really a theologian either. I'm merely an interested party who has read a little and thought a lot about these things."

"I'm not sure I know how to respond to you. If I cannot name this thing—"

"—Not a thing. A thing can be named because it has limits."

"All right. The whatever or *je ne sais quoi*."

"Not quite. A *je ne sais quoi* is completely unknown, but the foundation of reason is at least known by analogy."

"Fine. Let's say a *je sais un morceau*."

"Better to switch to German and say '*grundlegung*.'"

This time it was my turn to reach for the bread. There was only one piece left. I nabbed it and hurriedly buttered it—laying it on rather thick.

"Fine. So you are saying that unless I eschew the existence of any comprehensive 'groundwork' or '*grundlegung*' I cannot authentically deny the existence of God?"

"Forget the word, 'god.' Let's be Jews or Muslims and simply refuse to say the word. In English it is transliterated G-d so that it cannot be pronounced. This is in keeping with those great traditions." She smiled.

"Of course, if you want to put it that way, then, of course, everyone must accept whatever it is. But is it enough for you if I say, 'p or not-p,' the principle of non-contradiction, is the groundwork of my system of logic?"

"Does the principle of non-contradiction exist?" I didn't like the way this was going. There was no more bread. When would our meal come?

"Conventionally."

"In no other way? How was it discovered?"

"It cannot be discovered because every thought pre-supposes its existence."

Then the wine came and was poured. Andrea picked up her glass of wine and took a deep sip.

* * *

I know I'm not as sharp as I might be in areas of religion because that certainly is not one of my specialties. But I was taken enough by Andrea's line of thought (primitive as it was) to pause and turn the conversation.

By the time the seafood and pasta arrived (a special dish for two) the talk had turned to her work. I watched Andrea lift her wineglass. The cut glass goblets filled with pale liquid were in keeping with her entire presence. Andrea's arms were very thin, but somehow I sensed that they might be as powerful as her arguments.

"No, I do find it interesting, otherwise I couldn't do it."

"But the people you come in contact with. Surely they do not know French and German like you do."

"Language is merely a skill. It denotes nothing more. It's kind of like learning how to ride a bike or work on a computer. There is really no intelligence in it. But it is a mistake to think that everyone you meet must engage you in the same way. Or that everyone you meet or *anyone* you meet will match your every need. On the contrary, it is my opinion that almost anyone I meet has something that I can truly interact with as an equal. That level of intercourse is authentic from my point of view so long as I am pure in my intentions.

"When I meet clients who run their various organizations, be it the National Medical Association— a group of African American physicians who were shunned from the American Medical Association so that they had to form their own professional group — or The Academy of Orthopedic Surgeons, or the National Association of Hardware Dealers, or the American Association of Alternate Energy— these are my present clients—I tell you honestly, I can find ways to interact with each honestly."

"But what if the American Nazi Party asked you to run their newsletter?"

"I wouldn't do it."

"What about the Tobacco Association Institute?"

"Nix."

"Well, then. What's the deciding principle?"

"Whether I can live with it. Is it something that offends me? Then no. Is it something that I want to attend the Christmas party? Well, I'm not a party person so I don't like many parties at all. Anyway, there is no 'lowly or exalted' to me. If it's legal and doesn't bother my conscience, then I'll take on the client."

About that time we were ready to take on dessert.

* * *

After dinner we exited the realm of intellectual repartee and headed to a music place, Blues Alley, that was only a short distance away. We sat together without talking and listened a little too long to the jazz bands that night. By the time we realized it, midnight had turned the corner and getting home would be a problem. I suggested we take a cab.

"That will be very expensive back to Silver Spring."

"No, I'll drive you, but my car is parked at Notre Dame-Loyola. It's only five miles or so from here so the fare won't be too bad. Besides, it will give you a chance to see the school."

So we took a cab to my school and got out and took a stroll. We hadn't gone far before a security person with a flashlight told us to stand still. We did as we were told, but when the guard got closer I recognized him as Joe Numbhara, one of my former students. "Joe, it's me," I said.

"Oh, Dr. Simon. I'm sorry, I didn't recognize you."

"No problem, Joe. Just taking a stroll around campus.

"Not much happening in the summer, eh, Joe?"

"No. That's why they tell us to be even more alert." Joe looked at me with those beautiful large Nigerian eyes of his. Joe was a student who worked so very hard at everything he did that you had to have a warm feeling towards him.

I played the tour guide for the high points of campus before taking Andrea home. We didn't say much on the ride back, but we did plan a return engagement for Saturday night.

I glided home. Time was moving at a different pace. I can't remember when I last walked into my house at 2am. But tonight not only did I get back much later than I had planned, but I really could have cared less. I just wanted to hold onto the evening.

It was then that I saw my light flashing on my answer phone. Out of blind habit I picked it up. Big mistake.

"Bad news, Peter." The voice was Saul's. "The grand jury met with Josh Kaplan today and afterwards they entered a judgment that the disappearance of Moses Levi is officially a homicide. There are no indictments—yet, but you can bet that in a high profile case like this one there will be soon. I'll see you tomorrow before your eight am meeting with the Duke of Omnium."

I played the message again. I didn't need to be told that I am one step away from being indicted for murder one. And it was all that son-of-a-bitch Josh Kaplan. I don't understand what drives that guy. Why does he want to get rid of me?

CHAPTER FOURTEEN

Josh Kaplan, Director of Common Action

September 21, 1998

WHAT AM I GOING to do about Moses Levi? I have successfully transitioned from our old structure of project coordinators to one of regional administration. The purpose of this move was to a system in which there was a centralized chain of command.

So many non-profits on the "left of center" are stigmatized by a persistent sense of anarchy. The real genius of Bill Clinton as President is that he has brought the Democratic Party back to the middle. Why should the Republicans get all the money and power that the Middle has to offer?

In ten minutes I will speak to Moses. He is the only one of the Senior Project Coordinators (under the old system) that still has an active project. I have done everything I can (almost) to transition him over to my way of doing business. I began by offering him New York, Connecticut, Rhode Island and Massachusetts for his territory. It would have suited him well. He could have flourished under my system.

But Moses was stubborn. He got this Humanity Hospital Case in his craw and then you couldn't get him off of it. I've done everything I could. I really have. I've threatened to eliminate his stipend from the organization. But apparently he doesn't need it. In his prior life, he was a big time corporate lawyer who hit it rich on one case and then retired. Maybe he has a lot socked away. I don't know. He doesn't come from rich parents. The private investigators proved that. They also estimated from the beater car he drives and his lack of the modern things in life: cable TV, cellular phone, grass cutting service, and so forth that he is living well below others in his suburban neighborhood. He has none of the normal frills of modern life.

Moses has no mortgage on his house, shops at the bargain food stores, wears the same clothes over and over again. The man has a low overhead so that even if he doesn't have that much money coming in on his retirement annuity, he can still make his nut. Therefore, I can't threaten him monetarily. The man is either just making it on a shoestring or he lives way beneath his means. Either way, I have no financial leverage on the guy.

Nothing else in Moses' background shows any illegal dealings of any sort. The guy was a straight arrow as a lawyer. He worked his butt off for his clients and he still enjoys a very good reputation in the main line legal community. I wish that it were otherwise so that I could use it to get rid of him. The man is a source of constant irritation.

Moses is on a mission. But why? What makes him tick? Where is his weakness? These questions plague me.

Then Marge opened my door. "Moses is finally here." Marge is a very good secretary. Marge understands my need for preciseness and accuracy. Moses is antithetical to all of these. He arrived one hour late for the interview.

Moses ambled in with his hair disheveled and in a hurry. "Sorry to have been so late. I was at the Superior Court. This case is really getting dicey."

"Moses, I appreciate your zeal, but you know that I have a very busy schedule." I tried to sound as formidable as possible, but it really is of little use with a man like Moses. The guy is so damned persistent. He's like a bull dog who'll get his teeth into you and won't let go no matter what.

"So I'm sorry. Let's get down to business if you're so busy." Moses set his ancient brief case down and turned to face me.

"Moses, what I want to talk to you about is the Humanity Hospital case and your so-called Fair Start Initiative."

Moses merely nodded his head as if to bid me continue. "It has occurred to me that this case is taking much longer than any of us imagined. You are the only senior project coordinator who has not transitioned to becoming a Regional Administrative Head."

"Not true. You're forgetting about Maria Lugones."

"Maria Lugones. I'd like to forget about her. The traitor." Maria Lugones left our organization for the Natural Resources Defense Fund. She didn't like our administrative changes and just left! I always knew that she was an ally to Moses. He'd leave, too, except for this Fair Start Initiative that he's tied up with. This is a popular program that has been receiving a lot of press and ergo is bringing the organization a lot of donations. If I ax Moses, then I'll lose a considerable amount of money.

What I'd really like to do is to find a way to take over Moses' project myself so that I could get rid of the grandstander and become the point person, myself. I know more about how to revise our public policy on Affirmative Action, anyway. Moses is way too extreme to be effective.

"No one who follows her conscience is a traitor," returned Moses. "I only wish that I had always been as strong as Maria."

"Well, I didn't schedule you into my busy day to talk about Maria, for heaven's sake. The reason I wanted to talk to you was concerning this crazy Humanity Hospital case. I think you are taking this in the wrong direction." For some reason, I could not look Moses directly in the eye. I began fiddling with my pre-Columbian miniature stone inlay cuff links that had been a gift from one of our donors. I moved the little bar up and down that keeps the links in place. Over and over again I toyed with the bar.

"What do you mean 'the wrong direction'? It's clearly the right direction. Here we have a national hospital chain that is woefully under-represented by minority and women hires in all the desirable positions, save for nursing—who, themselves, are underpaid according to the measure of 'prevailing wage.' This is the perfect case that meets our mission as an organization. If you don't think so, I'd be happy to take my position to the Board for their direct approval."

Now I could look him directly in the eye. "You'd like that, wouldn't you? Another chance to try and show me up. That's what you're really all about, isn't it? The Moses Levi Show. Come and watch Moses and his magic tricks. Come one and come all."

"What is this really about, Josh?"

"Control. It's about control of this non-profit organization. There cannot be two leaders. I have been selected by the Board to be the Director. *Me* not *you*, Moses. I was the one selected."

"I never ran, Josh. You were the one who lobbied for the position since you came on board. You were selected and we all recognize your authority. But you must never forget that authority is not an external trapping. You must create authority from within. To be a leader is to be a servant. No one who is interested in power need apply. The best are those who are the most humble."

"What is this bullshit? Moses, you are really full of bullshit, do you know that? If I wanted to, I could have you fired like that." I snapped my fingers loudly in a bold, effective gesture. Then I pointed my index finger in a menacing way right at his ugly face. "I'm sick and tired of you and your parade. If we keep supporting you in your crusade against Humanity Hospitals, then you will have to submit to some supervision."

"Supervision? By whom? By you?"

"Don't act as if it were ridiculous. There are no cowboys in this organization. Each of us must submit our pet ideas to the will of the group. The community is greater than any of us and that is the way it should be. It is the community and not your personal ego that is first around here."

"And what about *your* ego, Josh?"

"I take that as an insolent and insubordinate comment."

"What is this? The Army? Really. Insolent. Insubordinate. I thought we were in the helping-others business."

"You don't understand, Moses. I am not asking you, I am telling you that your activities concerning the Humanity Hospitals lawsuit and the entire Fair Start Initiative will from this moment forward be overseen by me. There is no room for compromise on this issue."

"And what do you mean by 'oversight'? Do you want reports or something or do you want a hand in how to handle things?"

This was promising. I knew that I had him. It was a victory. Moses would always fold when pushed against it. And I was the one to push him.

Look at him over there, niggling in his seat. What would he be without my organization? If he thought that he could carry on without me, he would. He'd play the card immediately. But he doesn't. This is because he *can't.*

I mean *really,* could he have been all that great a lawyer if he's working at a little non-profit like Common Action? He was a senior partner at one of the top law firms in Washington, D.C. and tried one of the highest profile cases. He was a genius, but then something must have happened. Maybe it was his wife dying. Maybe he had a drug habit or something. Who knows? Our private detectives could find nothing, but that doesn't prove that he didn't snap. After all, even the best private dicks can't find everything.

My guess is that the guy snapped when his wife died or maybe he was working so hard that he went over the edge. Therefore, I'm dealing now with a shell of a man. A shell of a man who should be no match for me.

"For the time being, 'oversight' will mean weekly reports and briefings about future developments in the case and in the Fair Start Initiative. We'll start there and see what happens."

"Briefings and reports I can live with. But it is absolutely essential that I retain control of my project."

"Moses. There are no more projects. That was the vocabulary of the old Common Action." I got up. I felt inspired. It was time to pontificate. "Today there are only organizational initiatives. 'Common Action' means working for the good of the group. It means that individually we are nothing, but collectively, we can not only survive—but endure." I moved about my conference room and its rich mahogany paneling. This was beautiful wood that was produced by workers in Borneo who used ancient methods that included holding the wood with their bare feet while they cured and prepared it for chiseling and detailed woodwork.

These ancient craftsmen had been recommended by one of our donors, Sally Grackel, who knows what she's talking about since she comes from the Grackel's of Haddom, Connecticut (who own one of the largest wood working consortia in the world). They used to have a large plant in Connecticut, but with U.S. wages and all, they had to out-source all the work to developing countries (who really need the work since unemployment is often at 30-40% in their countries).

I was able to get a great deal for the organization of creating uniform conference rooms in all of our new regional offices that matched the newly created home office conference room. Fifteen thousand each. They were worth thirty. Sally told me about a similar contract that provided the same furnishings for over thirty-three thousand each!

I walked to the corner and fingered the carved designs with my fingers. They were imitations of a famous design in the Palace of Versailles that is forbidden to be photographed. (The only way Sally was able to get the pattern was from someone who sneaked inside and *drew* the designs by hand.)

And none of the trees were in endangered rain forests!

"So you see that though I am willing to adopt this compromise that you have suggested, I cannot promise that it will last forever. We need to eliminate cowboys from our organization. No collective agency can exist with vigilante outriders. It is important to create a situation in which *all* of the parts move in the same direction and in harmony.

"There is only one distraction to harmony at the moment, and that is *you*." I gathered myself for a momentous effect. My face was almost touching a carved mahogany flower. I was on such a roll that I no longer saw it as 'carved.' Everything was real. I poised to spin and confront my adversary. Now he would finally understand. "Moses—" I began as I turned. But the words caught in my throat as I saw that my quarry was gone. Moses had already left. Everything suddenly became awkward. My arm jerked forward in my abortive effort to make my point as my precious pre-Columbian cuff link dislodged and crashed to the table, spilling its precious stone in the process.

"Damn you, Moses. This is all your fault!"

THE JOURNAL OF MOSES LEVI: JUNE 6, 1992

From the Mishnah. 1A Yoma 8:9 — Transgressions between a human and G-d — the Day of Atonement atones. Transgressions between a human and his companion — the Day of Atonement does not atone until he has satisfied his companion.

1B Rabbi Elazar ben Azarian interpreted: "From all your sins before THE LORD, you will be cleansed" [Lev 16:30]: transgressions between a human and G-d — the Day of Atonement atones; transgressions between a human and his companion — the Day of Atonement does not atone until he has satisfied his companion.

2 *Leviticus 16:29. And this shall be a law for you forever: In the seventh month on the tenth day of the month, you shall afflict your souls and do no work at all, neither the citizen nor the resident alien in your midst. 30. Because on that day atonement will be made for you to cleanse you from all your sins: before THE LORD you will be clean.*

Levinas' Commentary.

3A 36-9/16-7. My sins in relation to G-d are forgiven without my depending on His good will! G-d is in one sense the OTHER par excellence, the other as other, the absolutely other—and nonetheless my disposition with this G-d depends only on me. The instrument of forgiveness is in my hands.

3B In contrast, the neighbor, my brother, a human, infinitely less other than the absolutely other is, in a certain sense, more other than G-d: to obtain his forgiveness on the Day of Atonement, I must as a precondition appease him. And if he refuses? As soon as there are two, everything is in danger. The other may refuse to forgive and leave me unforgiven. . . .

If I understand these passages correctly, then my expiation for my life as a big time corporate lawyer defending Waste Disposal and thwarting the proper execution of justice may be (in G-d's eyes) merely an act of contrition on Yom Kippur. But that is not the end of the story. No. I must also receive forgiveness from those I have injured. The texts seem to be very clear on this point. I cannot be forgiven of my sin against other people (from the human point of view) unless THOSE VERY PEOPLE who I have injured forgive me. Fifteen hundred and two people died. Imagine how many people were affected—at least five to ten times that amount. How can I personally confront fifteen thousand people?

CHAPTER FIFTEEN

Peter Simon

July 14, 2000

8:00 ANTE MERIDIAN. I can't believe I woke up at all. The contrast between my evening with Andrea and Saul's phone message was very jarring. I tell you honestly, one of the primary reasons I went into academia was the freedom it afforded. Freedom is very important to me. I don't know how I could cope if they convicted me. I'm not so naïve as to think innocence has much to do with it in cases such as this. The real jury is public opinion. If the public is against you, then it's a lynching—unless you're loaded. Unfortunately, I'm not. But I do have Saul Sani.

"Peter, we must move quickly." Saul had called me into his beach house—I mean office—to discuss our strategy. I sat in one of the beach chairs and listened to the eight compact discs that Saul had continuously playing. They were sounds of his favorite beaches. No people. Just water, sand, and breeze. On Saul's desk was a device that was a glass rectangular box that looked like a see-saw moving up and down, distributing the interior contents of two sorts of fluid back and forth slow, rhythmic motion.

"What do you want me to do?" I asked.

"I've scheduled a Press Conference at the National Press Club at noon. At that time you are going to outline the continuation of Moses' court case and the Fair Opportunity Initiative. It will all be very organic since we've been running it out of this office since mid-March and since Ulanda Washington, who was Moses' deputy counsel, will be our lead counsel."

"Have you written my speech for me?"

Saul laughed. He took off his glasses. "You read my mind, Peter. I tell you, it's a pleasure working with you." Then he put his glasses back on. "The speech is just a draft. I composed it early this morning with the Duke."

"Shall I look at it?"

"Look at it? Hell you've got to memorize it. You can add your own touches, of course, but we have to work on presentation and mock questions and answers."

"All that in four hours? I don't see how that will be possible," I said

"Four hours nothing," said Saul. "You've got three hours tops. And that's not counting breaks."

"Three hours! Impossible."

"Look, Peter. I love you. You're a great guy, but sometimes you're thick as a brick. In three hours you become ready or my friend, you've got an inside track for a murder one conviction." Then Saul took off his glasses again. "How does spending the rest of your life in jail feel, Peter?"

"I'd rather spend the three hours."

Saul nodded his head.

I turned to go, but I was stopped again. "Oh, one more thing, we need for you to bring the new girl you are dating to the press conference."

"What?" I spun around so fast I almost fell down.

"Your new girl. Call her. We need her at the Press Club at 11:30."

"What are you talking about? What girl? How do you know?"

"Remember I told you about Takoma Park and all that?" Saul was now picking up some papers on his desk in an obvious attempt to rid himself of me.

"But that was a random try. Everyone knows that you generally fail in random sample trials."

"Go to your rehearsal, Peter. I've got things to do here."

I turned to go as instructed, then stopped yet one more time. "Unless you had me followed. Saul, did you have me followed?"

"Good-bye, Peter," he said, as he dove beneath a wave of paperwork and became invisible.

*   *   *

The Duke of Omnium had finished with Ulanda. She had gone already. It was my turn. First, I had to read the script to myself. It wasn't very long. Then I had to read it out loud once to the Duke. Then I had to summarize as much as I could without the script. I was a miserable failure at this last stage.

"How's your vision?" asked the Duke.

"Well, I wear glasses as you can see."

"I mean with the glasses on, naturally."

"I'm far sighted."

"Far sighted? Excellent. Then you can use a teleprompter. I've put your entire speech up on a teleprompter that I've set aside here. Give me a hand to put it on the table." We lugged a portable teleprompter and set it up on the table. Then we plugged it into the laptop computer that would send out the images through some program or other.

I stood up behind the table and we worked on my optimum distance to stand and speak without my glasses. Two and a half feet seemed to be perfect. I could read the seventy-five point type like a pro.

"Look," I said. "There are a few changes I'd like to make here."

"What changes?" asked the Duke.

"Well, for starters, all this stuff about how happy I was when Moses asked me to come on board. That is false. I was rather miffed at Moses because he took my steady girl away from me in college."

"And you want to tell the world about that, do you?"

"I guess not."

"Of course not. What else?"

"Then there is the issue of Senator Blight. I don't really like him. Must I form an alliance with him? I mean the man is a joke, to progressive sort of people like myself. This will make me a laughing stock."

The Duke took out a cigarette, lit it, and took a deep draw. Then he shook his head. "You really *are* a bit of a novice, aren't you?"

"Okay. I see. Self-interest. Do you want to sleep with a whore—no better to say do you want to become a whore in order to save your skin. But what about your soul?"

The Duke smiled, took another deep draw and exhaled it via his nostrils. "Peter, our dossier on you says that you are an atheist. What do you care about your goddamn soul?"

"You're right, of course. But lately. . . I'm rather confused. Lately—very recently, I've started to consider—"

"Well, stop considering. Considering will get you electrocuted—or possibly the more humane lethal injection. That's the penalty for murder in your tri-state area."

"The District of Columbia is not a state."

"Still splitting hairs. You are a philosopher to the core."

"Must I do everything you say?"

"Look, Peter. Time is rather short. You must change the paradigm here. On the one hand you want to pull out your hair about every little bit of quibble. That was the way you were professionally trained. I can appreciate that. But few people in the general public do. To them you philosophers are infected with a sort of disease. It is a mental disorder that makes you find unnecessary complication in everything. You are an outcast in your philosopher persona. Ditch it or die."

"Thank God for that. Do you know Plato's depiction of the general populace in that section of the *Republic* commonly known as 'The Cave' and 'The Divided Line'?"

"Do you remember Aristophanes' treatment of Socrates?" The Duke surprised me with his erudition.

"Yes. He made Socrates out to be a pettifogger."

"Exactly. And what did they do to Socrates?"

I winced. "What should we do now?"

One more long drag. The cigarette was almost finished. "I need for you to call your honey and tell her to come to the National Press Club by 11:30."

Again, I hesitated. It was one thing to prostitute my individual values in order to save my own skin, but I didn't like pulling Andrea into this. I genuinely liked Andrea. She was the most authentic thing that has happened to me since Sarah Z. How could I ask someone I truly valued for herself to be used only for the sake of my salvation? Wouldn't this mean that I would be viewing her as an object for my sole benefit? Wouldn't this be violating Kant's third form of the categorical imperative that sanctioned using another as a 'means only'? "I'm not sure whether that would be a right thing to do. I do respect Andrea. I don't want to treat her as merely some bibelot that has camera value."

Then the Duke surprised me. Instead of his flip replies, the man extinguished his cigarette and got up from his chair and approached me. "Peter," he said without veneer. "Peter, that's one of the central reasons why powerful forces are on your side. All we ask is that you don't screw it up by indulging yourself in one of those philosophical flights of fancy."

"That's how it is viewed, isn't it? You don't have to answer. I know." I would never have a chance to have a relationship with Andrea if I were in prison—not to mention on death row for a crime I did not commit. Therefore, I decided at that moment to reach into my pocket and take out my diary on which I'd written Andrea's phone number. "Give me the phone. I'll make the call."

*   *   *

Strangely enough, Andrea thought it would be fun. She'd never been to the National Press Club before. I promised to take her out to lunch afterwards. However, something still bothered me about using Andrea as a prop to undercut the District Attorney's case against me on the "scorned man" point. I know that I would be less bothered by this if I didn't really feel something genuine for Andrea. I desperately want this to work. I have not had luck with women. Probably 'luck' is the wrong word to use. Another term such as 'success' that denotes dessert would probably be better. I'm probably a self-centered louse when it comes right down to it.

But maybe people can change?

At any rate, it was my turn to change. The Duke had hired a very nice suit of clothes for me. There was someone coming in to do my hair and apply make-up. I was preparing for the rôle of my life.

*   *   *

I met Andrea at the Press Club. She looked very excited. "Hey Peter, nice suit," she said, stroking the rented threads. "What's the occasion?"

"A press conference on the Fair Opportunity Initiative."

"But isn't that movement run by Moses something or other?"

"Levi. Moses Levi."

"Yes, that's right, but wait—isn't he the one who just disappeared? The authorities think it's murder. I heard it on the radio this morning."

"Right again, but he can't very well run his movement if he has been murdered, now, can he?"

Andrea didn't answer. Her face showed her perplexity.

"Look, I know—or knew—Moses Levi because he and I were roommates in college—at Pembroke."

"Moses Levi went to Pembroke?"

"Absolutely. He was a philosophy major."

"Just like you."

"Yes, we had a number of things in common."

Andrea shook her head in amazement. "So now you are picking up his cause to keep it going. That's very noble of you." Andrea took my arm and gave it a squeeze as she said this.

Then Martin, Saul's secretary who was leading me around, told me to get into another room. Martin had a very high and lilting voice that made you think that he might be a push over. But Martin was anything but a push over. He was a human dynamo (perfectly suited for that nuclear power plant of a boss, Saul). Martin stood about 5'9" and was very slight of build with unusually long fingers. Those fingers gripped my shoulder and hurried me away. Andrea followed.

In the antechamber, or green room, we waited for our cue. Martin was very nervous. He kept combing his rapidly thinning hair away from his twenty-something brow. We went over my speech a couple of times and how I might retrieve my glasses from my inside coat pocket should I need them.

There was something about this hustle bustle that I rather liked. It was certainly different from anything I'd ever experienced before. Even the press conference four months earlier with Moses when he sandbagged me was not anywhere near the production this was. I had to believe that there were interests at stake here that I could not imagine.

Then I was given the cue. I smiled. Andrea smiled. Martin smiled. We all strode forward. Within a blur of activity and flashing lights my smile was before the American people.

"Good afternoon," I began. "I'd like to begin by reading a prepared statement." Then I took a folded copy of some pages printed just that day from the Dairy Association's website on the best way to prepare cheddar cheese. This was in case I forgot and left my notes on the podium. There would be no secret information at hand. It also gave the television audience the impression that I had written and was about to deliver my own speech. Everything is impressions. Is this related to the appearance vs. reality question?

I did a good job. I felt fine about reading from the teleprompter. My cadence was not hurried. I gestured at just the right times and I felt interaction with my audience. When my talk was over, there was a buzz of noise and a new popping of lights.

"Dr. Simon will now entertain a few questions from the floor."

With the lights in my face I was not readily able to see my questioners.

"Yes," began a female voice without a body. "Is it true that you are a reluctant addition to this movement?"

Now I know what they meant about not engaging in philosophical analysis. My first instinct was to ask what was meant by "reluctant." I could honestly say that I was indeed reluctant about joining Moses for various personal reasons but I was not reluctant about supporting this position. It was a rather divided question. However, this was one of the questions we had practiced so I said without a pause, "Absolutely not! If you look at my published writings in ethics you will find that I have always supported Affirmative Action and have, myself, suggested some of the modifications that Moses Levi has proposed."

At that moment, two assistants named Bonnie and Connie started handing out excerpts from my published articles on these issues.

"Isn't it true that you hated Moses Levi and that your hatred went so far as to cause you to strike him just outside a prominent District of Columbia restaurant?"

I laughed. We had practiced this laugh seventeen times before getting it right. I executed the laugh perfectly. "Moses Levi and I were college roommates. As anyone knows who has been close to his college roommate, there are little hot buttons that each person knows about. Moses and I were engaged in some discussion when one of those little hot buttons was pressed, and I hit him. I'm sorry I hit him, but he pressed the button knowing what I'd do—If I'd pressed one of his hot buttons, perhaps he'd have hit me!"

Bonnie and Connie handed out a circular about how Moses and I had been life-long friends.

"So how hot is this trigger temper of yours, Dr. Simon? Is it hot enough to kill?"

This was way out of bounds as far as I was concerned. We did not practice this question. "I would not say that I had a hot trigger temper at all. I can't really see you Ms.?"

"Guber. Ms. Shelly Guber, Flagstone Magazine—internet, you know."

"Of course, Ms. Guber. But there *are* some gender-linked activities that many may not understand. Boys hitting boys, men hitting men. This happens. It is not unusual among close friends in the male gender. Women may interpret their love,aggression differently. I don't know. Philosophical feminism is not my specialty. But I do know that some prominent feminists do make this argument."

"So what are you saying, Dr. Simon?"

"I'm saying that some symbolic interactions that are perfectly normal among some men can be misinterpreted by those unaccustomed with these customs. There is a rich literature on this topic that you can find on the Philosophers Index and on Dialogue—both are readily available electronically. But in a fairly simplistic way, let me say that Moses, let's hope he's still alive, and myself are as close as two men can be—without being homosexual, of course."

I don't know why I mentioned the homosexual bit, but I know that so many people get the wrong impression when you mention friendship between men.

"Dr. Simon. Can what you say really be true given that Moses Levi stole your fiancée from you while you were both in college?"

This one we'd practiced. "That was a long time ago. I was never engaged to Sarah Zipporah Wolfe. We dated but like many college romances, it did not go any further. If I were to ask the same question to you of the press corps, how many could say that they never broke up with anyone in college? Did it preoccupy you? Of course not. This is rather ridiculous. In America, college romances are like the morning frost, beautiful while they last, but very temporal."

This last answer was very effective. Bonnie and Connie began circulating statistics on college romances showing that fewer than 10% ever end up in marriage. There were a few more noise level questions. But in essence we were through.

Then was the time for the group picture. Andrea stepped forward, unasked, and stood beside me. Saul appeared from nowhere and then there was also Ulanda Washington. A perfect scene. A perfectly executed drama.

The revenge question had been met head on. And the scorned man (old case) had been addressed directly as well as the unasked (new case) of a scorned man.

I was thankful to my handlers. They had acted intelligently. We walked off the stage and back into the anteroom. Everyone was very excited. It was a euphoric atmosphere when Martin came to me and said quietly, "We've got to get out of here now. At this moment across town, Josh Kaplan has just begun his counter news conference."

I was stunned. Perhaps because of all the buzz and effort, I wanted to bask in the afterglow. But facts are facts. This bulldog Josh Kaplan had something in his craw that he could not relinquish.

THE JOURNAL OF MOSES LEVI:
SEPTEMBER 10, 1992

The Babylonian Talmud

4A Yoma 87a. "Transgressions between a human and God, etc.": R. Joseph bar Havu raised an objection to R. Abbuhu: "Transgressions between a human and his companion—the Day of Atonement does not atone?" But it is written: 'If a man sin against a man, God will mediate.' [1 Sam 2:25]

4B) "What does Elohim mean? The judge."

4C) "Then how do you interpret the conclusion: 'And if a man sin against THE LORD, who will mediate for him?"

4D) "This is what is says: 'If a man sins against a man and appeases him—God will forgive him; and if a man sins against THE LORD—who can appease? Only repentance and good deeds.'"

5 Samuel 2:25. "If a man sin against a man, God will mediate; but if against THE LORD, who will mediate for him?" But they did not listen to the voice of their father because THE LORD was pleased that they should die.

Levinas' Commentary

6A. 42-43/19 But the gemara decidely rejects this position. Here is the version it proposes: [Levinas' translation] "If a man commits a sin against a man and appeases him—God will forgive him; but if the sin is against God—who can intercede for him? Only repentance and good deeds. . . The solution consists of inserting the italicized words, into the Biblical verse, to bend it to the spirit of the Mishnah. One could not be less attached to the letter and more enamored of the spirit.

6B). It is thus very serious to have offended a human. Forgiveness depends on him, one finds oneself in his hands. There is no forgiveness that has not been requested by the guilty. The guilty must recognize his sin; the offended one must want to welcome the supplications of the offender. Moreover, no one can forgive, if he has not had forgiveness requested by the offender, if the guilty has not sought to appease the offended.

Powerful stuff. Forgiveness is an intimate human interaction between two individuals. There are two parties: the person who has offended (A) and the person who has been injured (B). A cannot be forgiven unless he solicits forgiveness from B and B agrees to forgive him. It is within B's discretion to forgive or not to forgive.

The converse situation is also interesting. B cannot forgive A—even if he wants to, unless A has solicited his pardon. Thus, even if B is willing to forgive A, he cannot do so unless A approaches him in contrition and solicits his forgiveness.

This whole model works fine on the level of a two-party interaction. But what happens when there is 1502 times ten—or more?

The Journal of Moses Levi: September 10, 1993
The Babylonian Talmud

4G) R. Hisda said: He needs to appease him with three lines of three people each, as it is said: "He lines up men and says, 'I have sinned and I have perverted what was right and it did not benefit me.'" (Job 33:27).

4H) R. Jose ben Hanaina said: Anyone who asks pardon of his companion does not ask him more than three times, as it is said: "Forgive, I pray you now . . . and now we pray you." (Gen 50:17).

4I) And if he died? He brings ten people and stands them by his grave and says: "I have sinned against the Lord, the God of Isreal, and against this one, whom I have wronged."

Job 33:26. "He will pray to God, and he will be favorable to Him. He will see His face in joy, for He renders to each man his righteousness. 27)

He lines up men and says, 'I have sinned and I have perverted what was right and it did not benefit me.'"

Genesis 50:16. *And they sent to Joseph saying, "Your father commanded before his death saying, 17) 'So shall you say to Joseph, "Forgive, I pray you please, the trespass of your brothers and their sin; for they did evil to you and now we pray you forgive, the trespass of the servants of God of your father."'" And Joseph wept as they spoke to him.*

Levinas' Commentary

11) 48-9/22. *In this passage there would be three entreaties or a ternary rhythm which would prove the thesis of Rab Jose bar Hanina. The commentators discuss its cogency. What does it matter? I would like to fasten on the choice of Biblical verse. What example of an offense was sought in the Bible for the occasion? The story of the brothers who sold their brother, Joseph, into slavery. The exploitation of man by man would therefore be the prototype of offense, imitated by all offenses (even verbal).*

I'm not sure this helps any. Look, the tradition says that if you sin against another, then you can receive forgiveness from God on the Day of Atonement (Yom Kippur). This is achieved by a contrite heart.

The situation with people is different. When you sin against your neighbor, it is in your neighbor's power to forgive you if you have petitioned him for forgiveness. [If you haven't petitioned him, then even your neighbor is powerless to forgive you.]

If your neighbor decides not to forgive you, then you may petition him three more times in the presence of three witnesses. Even then your neighbor may refuse to grant you forgiveness. But this is a limited power. The limit is one's lifetime. When your neighbor dies, the weight of your guilt may finally be relieved by bringing ten people to the grave and repeating your petition for forgiveness.

A person cannot persist in his refusal to forgive if he is dead. The weight of sin should be lifted. What is necessary to lift this weight is a public acknowledgment of guilt to ten people at the grave site. When this occurs, then forgiveness is automatic. Nothing comes easy. But there are some things you can't take with you. The animosity of hatred is one of these.

THE JOURNAL OF MOSES LEVI:
SEPTEMBER 10, 1995

It seems to me that I have read and studied enough on this topic. It is apparent to me that one way to forgiveness is to petition THE LORD. I have done this.

But becoming at one with humankind is another issue. The wisdom literature tells me that the principal model of forgiveness is based upon a model of one person wronging another. This was (and perhaps is) its principle source of wrong doing. From this model, I could try to find a way to solicit the forgiveness of the families that I wronged. They might take it the wrong way and sue me, but I created a trust several years ago when I became a pro bono attorney in order to protect my livelihood. I do not believe my assets are at risk.

If the families I have wronged will not forgive me or will simply not answer, then I will have to create a database and find out when the closest living relative dies and solicit forgiveness at the funeral (or shortly thereafter so as not to disrupt the ceremony).

But clearly there are too many to really do this. This is impossible. Really, 20,000 funerals? Tracking that many people and maybe more? It's impossible.

What recourse is there for crimes against Humanity? Haven't I, a Jew, found myself in the situation that faces the Nazis? I have been an accessory to a crime against Humanity. Many Nazis were active agents and the rest accessories to such crimes, as well. We are really in the same dilemma. We have injured so many that we cannot possibly ever discover forgiveness in the traditional means. It is closed to us.

There is always the old standard of good works and trusting in the Lord. But there is a lot of uncertainty in that. Nothing is guaranteed. But perhaps that is all I deserve. What happiness faces the 1,502 souls that died and whose families were not compensated because I defended Waste Disposal so bravely (knowing in my heart they were guilty)?

Can there be forgiveness for a crime against Humanity? Is this just the sort of crime that is forever unforgiven? When I think of the Nazis I feel satisfaction at this thought. When I think of my own situation, I feel terror.

CHAPTER SIXTEEN

Josh Kaplan

March 15, 2000

THE SINGLE TRAIT that marks a successful leader from an unsuccessful leader is the ability constantly to engage in strategic thinking. By strategic thinking I mean the ability to always have the big picture in front of you and a list of intermediate steps that will lead to that goal. In this way, whenever confronted by a novel situation, one can merely say to himself, "Does this promote my ultimate designs?" If it does, then one follows that path. If it doesn't, then one rejects it.

In this way there is no superfluous misdirection. Success depends upon controlling the misdirection. You know where you want to get. Any sub-action will either aid you in getting there or hinder you from getting there or is neutral. Nothing short of a positive step forward should be adopted.

This is the bible that I've lived by and, believe-you-me, it has tumbled the walls of Jericho. I can tell you. I have moved our endowment from 12 million dollars in 1996 to over 150 million. That in only four years! Nobody has helped our organization as much. When I took over we were dipping into our endowment each year because there was such lax oversight on the budget. Almost anything counted as a reason to commit more funds.

That had to stop. And it did when I took over.

I have really gotten this foundation into incredible shape since assuming command. Our record keeping is so good that we could withstand the most stringent audit whenever and wherever it was demanded. This is outstanding for a small foundation like Common

Action. We have also instituted an institutional effectiveness program that tracks what we do each business quarter and matches that to our institutional mission and our strategic plan. In this way we can show our donors just how well we are doing as measured against what we say we are doing.

My work has been very rewarding to me—except for one continued irritant: Moses Levi. Moses has not taken the cue that he is no longer welcomed as a part of Common Action. I would have gotten rid of him long ago except for one thing: the Humanity Hospital Case. Moses really seemed to fall into a big case with Humanity. I mean, it involves the entire attitude that our country has towards Affirmative Action and redress of unethical treatment towards minorities.

On the surface this is a good case for us. Not a great case (too controversial), but an *acceptable* case. This is the reason why I allowed us to continue. It was just high enough in the public consciousness that I could not let it go. It was our highest profile case. An organization like ours needs high profile cases in order to attract donors. Without money no non-profit can survive. And we did attract many donors because of the case. Not a month went by without positive buzz from the case (or Moses' other effort to create a national dialogue on the topic) making the major news media. Therefore, I gave this Moses some slack.

I tell you; it was a mistake.

Moses refused to accept any direction from me. He was late on the reports that we had agreed upon and after a year or so stopped submitting them entirely. It was at that point that I pulled the plug and cut off his stipend from our organization. It didn't matter. I knew it wouldn't matter. I had commissioned extensive background checks on all our senior employees and I knew this son-of-a-bitch better than he knew himself. He was living off some pathetic stipend so that he could be some sort of free spirit. Well, I can tell you what I think of that. Here you have this man who pretended to be a "man of the people." Yet he lives off the interest of money he made as a big time corporate lawyer. How can you pretend to change? Once a pawn of the wealthy, always a pawn of the wealthy—unless, of course, he agrees to give away all the money he made as a lawyer in order to "purify" himself. Better a splash in the Jordan River, I'd say. But anyway, I see this as the height of hypocrisy. He *says* on the one hand, "I am an advocate of the common man—especially those who are oppressed by our present system (minority groups)." On the other hand, he *acted* by having worked for a high-powered corporate law firm that has as its *raison d'être* screwing the little guy so that the powerful might continue to increase their influence. How can he have it both ways?

It just makes me sick.

I'll tell you that I have tried to make his life difficult. I have taken him off the senior staff so that he cannot attend our meetings and know just exactly what we are doing (though I suspect that Ulanda Washington is filling him in now that Maria Lugones is gone). How does one run an organization when there is disloyalty in the ranks? I've kept my eye upon Ulanda for some time. She is not a team player. I mean, our name is 'Common Action.' If that doesn't mean submerging one's own personal ego to the common purpose, then I don't know what does. I'm a great Michael Sandel and communitarian fan. These forward-thinking souls set forth that it is the good of the community that takes precedence over individual inclinations. This is absolutely essential if anything of importance is to happen.

At any rate, Ulanda is probably a traitor to the cause. I've already taken care to eliminate her from sensitive memos. However, I'm not as stupid as some might think. I've created plants of my own: Sam Rodriguez, Jane Eliot and Ayanna Smith. I have the entire staff under my thumb, except for Washington. I've cut off Moses' salary from the foundation, but have continued some minor staff support. I assume the bulk of the money necessary to keep things going has come from Saul Sani. I don't know what's in it for him, but he must have an angle.

Well, anyway, I set up Sam, Jane, and Ayanna as *my* plants to counteract the influence of Ulanda. They give me weekly reports on the inside scoop of what's going on with Moses. The only way that I can keep up with his tricks is to have adequate information. If I know what Moses is doing, then perhaps I can ensure that he will not embarrass this organization. This is no mere dream. Last month, both *Time* and *Newsweek* ran articles on Moses and his Fair Opportunity Initiative.

Moses wants to modify Affirmative Action so that both upper income minorities and lower income Caucasians can benefit from government assistance. His idea is to mix economic need and societal disadvantage to create a continuing program that is based upon natural desert (servicing the traditional crowd of indigent minorities along with this new emphasis). The popular editors of those publications were effusive in their praise. However, there was very little copy on Common Action—some, but not enough. Mainly, it was all about Moses. It was enough to make you sick. I wasn't mentioned once in either article.

The more I thought about those articles, the more I was convinced that it was time to take over Moses' project. I had ample reason to take his project away from him due to his failure to deliver the proper progress reports that I had insisted upon (in writing). No one could find fault with *me.*

I instructed my secretary to get Moses on the phone. It was a day later by the time that I could confront that no-good grandstander. I made it perfectly clear in my call that he had failed the organization. We have our rules and he had flaunted them. He reminded me that there was a 90-day notice period for termination in his employment contract that ran from the first of the month. This meant that the earliest I could get rid of his sorry ass was July 1st.

I ground my teeth but realized that there was really nothing that I could do. We agreed that by midnight of June 30th, Moses would be history. I would take over his operation.

Moses made a few nasty comments about my lack of legal experience and the fact that I was admitted to the bar in D.C. rather recently (just in case I might need it). I had been admitted to the Wisconsin Bar six months after my graduation from Marquette University Law School. The fact that I chose to serve the public instead of making myself rich shouldn't count against me. In fact, most people in this organization would say that it was a telling point in favor of *my* priorities and moral character.

You know, sometimes I wonder whether it is really just an ego thing with this Moses. I mean that he has now associated himself with one of the most visible cases on the popular scene. The only reason it is so popular is that he has been full of self-promotion at every step. It's so egregious that sometimes I wonder whether the son-of-a-bitch is grooming himself for public office. I wouldn't put it past him. Moses would do anything to promote Moses.

When I think of the mission statement that I wrote for Common Action and its emphasis upon everyone bending his ego to the common good, I almost can't believe that we have a Moses Levi in our organization!

Well, that will be over in 90 days or so. After June 30th there will be no more Moses Levi associated with Common Action, and though the man might have enough scratch to keep his body and soul together without an income from us (long gone), he does not have enough to carry on his program without our support. When the money for his staff, court filings, and other expenses is gone, then Moses is history.

It will be so nice to be permanently rid of the guy. He has always irritated me. In so many ways he has irritated me. First there is his hauteur. Second there is his "holier than thou" attitude. Third there is his "I wear my Jewishness on my sleeve" attitude. I'm just as Jewish as he is—more so. I'm Conservative. He's Reform: Jew in name only. He can't pull the religion card on me. I'm better than he is in that score.

Lastly is the way that the guy seems to move at his own pace and get everything he wants. This is what bothers me the most. I bust my butt to get where I am. I do everything by the rules, and this Moses goes at *his* own pace and seems to obey no one on this earth.

The man does not deserve to live. His time has come and gone. I have already sketched out a transition team that will shadow Moses every day from here on out in order to ensure that he doesn't try to pull something else. I'll have my people taking over from his people the day-to-day operations of the legal suit so that come July 1st we will be up to speed and able to continue without pausing.

One-by-one I will replace his staff with *my* people. I will wait and replace Sam last so that I can continue to get intelligence on how Moses intends to thwart my initiatives—for I am certain that he will continue to try to get his way. His ego is too big to fall over and play dead. No. That is too much for even me to dream for.

What is needed instead is some sort of strategic action plan that will put into effect what is only a dream at present. In order to get rid of Moses, I will have to be one step ahead of him with the power to check his every move. But more than that. I have to make it my mission to get rid of Moses Levi forever. The man is a burden. I don't like burdens.

CHAPTER SEVENTEEN

Peter Simon

July 14, 2000

I SUPPOSE the modern age is a blessing and a curse. The blessing is that the technology allows us to save and extend life. The curse is that communications move so quickly that Josh Kaplan is able to stage a news conference only thirty minutes after we finish. Apparently it was all in the cards because another cadre of reporters was at his corporate headquarters full of his lunch spread and fine wine to lob softball questions to this bastion of public interest.

I found all this out when I returned with Andrea to Saul's Ballston office. We waited in the conference room with Martin who was going over the press conference with me in a technical sort of way. "Your eyes picked up the principal camera every time, Peter. That was very well done. When one is unsure, you get the Richard Nixon effect of shifting eyes. What the American people like least are shifting eyes."

I nodded.

Martin was very animated about these small details. I suppose that he was hired to be a small detail man. Somebody has to do it. I know that I'm not very good at it.

I was then summoned out of the room to take a phone call from the Duke. I went into a smaller conference room to take the call.

"Decent job, Peter," said the Duke. "Sorry we didn't anticipate that one question, but you handled it fine. In the other press conference, Josh Kaplan has vowed to carry on the Fair Opportunity Initiative under his direction."

"What? That little scoundrel."

"Don't worry. I had information that he was going to do this so I had prepared a statement from you welcoming any and all organizations that want to assist you. This statement was released to the press one minute before Josh's press conference.

"Oh, thanks for telling me."

"In the meantime, I have arranged for S.O.S to be our host organization. They will be holding a press conference in ninety minutes. I want you to be there standing by. Oh, be sure to take Andrea with you."

There was a pause. "Is that all?" I asked.

"Enough for now. See you tomorrow at eight."

"Tomorrow's Saturday."

"Right. See you at eight."

*   *   *

Andrea was already ready to go. I looked at her apologetically. She only smiled. I knew that I had to take her to dinner.

S.O.S. (Save Our-Selves) is a quirky non-profit that operates out of Alexandria. S.O.S. has been associated in the past with groups like Greenpeace and Amnesty International. It has a real cosmopolitan flavor that ranges from the left to the far left. However, they have also been collateral supporters of mainstream groups like Habitat for Humanity and The Salvation Army.

We drove down the George Washington Parkway past Washington National Airport along Route 1 into Alexandria. I always get a queer sense driving into old town Alexandria. Aside from Boston, Williamsburg, and Philadelphia, it has the most Colonial feel of any American city. From the red brick sidewalks to the rolling timbered shops and buildings that are ever so slightly continuing to settle on the hills that descend towards the Potomac River, the town makes you feel as if you were in a different time. It would almost seem natural to see Thomas Jefferson or George Washington stroll out of a tavern with a glow on their cheeks and a twinkle in their eyes.

It was here that S.O.S. had its headquarters.

Andrea, Martin, and I mounted the steep steps to the second story and a rather smallish ballroom that had been the jewel of the former mansion once occupied by some blue blood. This ballroom would be the site of the press conference. The floorboards were very wide and warped in places. The glass in the windows was old, wavy and distorted the outside world. Warped distortions seemed to be the perfect venue for a press conference.

We were greeted by the director, Miriam Batmanghli, an Iranian émigré. "Welcome, Peter, Andrea, and Martin. We've been expecting you. I can't tell you how excited we are about becoming the lead organization in the Fair Opportunity Initiative. It will be a breakout event for our organization and we feel strategically placed to be able to present this agenda to the American People in a forceful way."

"Thank you," I said.

Martin closeted himself with Miriam for a moment and then hurried us off to a small room at the other end of the hall. The press conference would be very small compared to our earlier one, but there were television cameras in place and seating for fifty or so.

"They want you to read this paragraph."

"Has it been approved?" I asked, not caring what Andrea might think.

"Yes. But there is no teleprompter here so you'll have to memorize it. You have four minutes. Get at it."

*   *   *

I got at it. This meant that I tried to follow the sense of it. I was never good at memorizing anything word for word. I have always substituted meaning for exactitude.

Though the group was much smaller, there were still the obnoxious lights and commotion.

We walked in, as before, however this time I was not center stage. Miriam was under the spotlight.

Miriam smiled graciously. One of her deputies delivered the opening remarks. Miriam was standing on the opposite side of the dais so that I could watch her as the remarks were being delivered. Miriam is a short, full figured woman who generates a sense of graciousness. I decided that Alexandria was a perfect home for her. Then I was pushed forward.

I smiled broadly and then remembered that I still had on my glasses that I had donned to read and memorize my speech. I turned and shook Miriam's hand. Then I faced the group of twenty reporters and took off my glasses in a bold gesture. Our claques were whooping it up a bit.

"I am here this afternoon to welcome S.O.S. as the heir to Moses Levi's Fair Opportunity Initiative. S.O.S. has long served humanity on almost every continent in the cause of human rights, the elimination of poverty, and the protection of the children of the world.

"These are the disenfranchised, the unprotected and the needy. It is therefore hardly surprising that S.O.S. would be chosen by Moses Levi's hand-picked lieutenants to carry the mantle into the Twenty-First Century." More applause.

"And so without further ado, let me present to you the woman who will help bring fair opportunity to all Americans and people everywhere, Miriam Batmanghli!"

I stepped back and Miriam glided past me. For a woman of her build she moved with exceeding grace. "Thank you," she said blowing kisses to our claques, who were now beside themselves. "You are so very generous. I am proud to accept the challenge of the Fair Opportunity Initiative and the help of Moses Levi's handpicked successors, Peter Simon and Ulanda Washington. With the help of Professor Simon and Counselor Washington we can initiate strategic alliances with organizations around the world who are interested in fair opportunity for all.

"Even as I speak, contacts have been made with organizations in India, Iran, Vietnam, and Korea who are willing to do what they can to add our agenda to their own. There is no 'ownership' to this cause. It is a cooperative effort among people of goodwill everywhere who want to bring about justice in the world.

"And so I hope you will join me in giving a rousing send off to this exciting mission. Fair opportunity for all! FAIR OPPORTUNITY FOR ALL!" Our claques began chanting, "Fair Opportunity for all." This went on for a few minutes until they decided it was safe to allow a few questions.

"Ms. Batmanghli, just a few hours ago across town, Josh Kaplan held a news conference in which he claimed to be the rightful heir to Moses Levi's crusade. After all, it was under the auspices of Common Action that Mr. Levi began Fair Opportunity in the first place."

"We welcome the help of Josh Kaplan and Common Action in this endeavor. However, it should be noted that Common Action fired Moses Levi in March and cut off all funding for his project. Since that time, Moses acted swiftly to bring in Peter Simon and some associates of his into the picture. It was these handpicked individuals who kept the Fair Opportunity Initiative going. Working without pay, Peter Simon and Ulanda Washington put principle above profit and helped steady a project that Common Action did not want.

"If Common Action has seen the error of their ways and wants to join up again, we'd be happy to bring them on board. This is not about ownership of anything. This about helping disadvantaged Native Americans, Latinos, African Americans and any other group that seems to have been shut out of the American Dream.

"We welcome Common Action or anyone who wishes to help make this vision a reality."

There were a few more questions of little consequence. Soon we were off the stage and in the back room. It was five o'clock. Andrea and I looked at each other. "They've got a lot of good restaurants in Alexandria. Do you want to have dinner?"

"It's a little early, but then we haven't had lunch. I haven't even had breakfast."

I put my arm around Andrea. There was much I needed to tell her. Dinner would be as good as any way to get to what needed to be said.

Andrea chose a Colonial chophouse. Inside it was very dark. There was air conditioning, but the timbers of the floor and ceiling lent a musty aroma that spoke of age. We sat at a roughhewn wooden table that had two tallow candles atop. We ordered an appetizer and a liter of red house wine and settled back.

"It was good of you to come today. I can't tell you how much my life has been in turmoil since Moses Levi chose me to help him in March."

"I know. I heard Miriam talk about it," said Andrea. "But the way I remember it from the press at the time, weren't you reluctant to help Moses?"

"I wasn't overjoyed to come on board. That's true. He knew I felt this way so he rather surprised me about the whole thing at a press conference—not too unlike the second one we had today."

"He just sprang it on you?"

"That's right. In front of the cameras was the first time I got an inkling of what he wanted to do. Naturally, I was a bit befuddled. Who wouldn't be? On the one hand, I wanted to support him. I mean, intellectually I am in favor of everything that he wants to do. But on the other hand, Moses and I had some unfortunate history together, too. He took the girl I had been dating in college away from me while I was away on a Pembroke's London Seminar in the fall term of my senior year."

"He took your girl away from you?"

"Yes."

"Wait. I'm no philosopher, but I'm a bit confused here. I know how someone can take your car away from you or a valuable book. But how can one take a person away from you? You don't own a person. She was never in your possession in the first place."

"This is true. I didn't own Sarah Z. But we had been dating since her freshman year. She was a year younger than I was."

"Were you engaged?"

"No. In my time, virtually no one got engaged at Pembroke. It just wasn't done."

"It still isn't," added Andrea.

Then the food and wine came. We pitched in and continued.

"Sarah and I weren't engaged, but we had an understanding that we probably would get married or live together after college—it all amounts to the same thing."

"Yes. I agree with you. Both are natural marriages. One is both a natural and a conventional marriage."

"Yes. But I thought it wasn't very nice of Moses to go after Sarah when I was away. I mean, I wouldn't have done it to him."

"But Sarah has a part in this, you know. No one can 'go after her' if she isn't inclined to let herself be 'gotten.'"

"You're right, of course. But somehow I've always felt more anger at Moses than at Sarah."

"Why?"

"I don't know."

There was a long pause. Andrea ate for a while and seemed absorbed in thought.

"You see, I wanted to tell you all this because I have dragged you into this and I wanted you to know and because—well, because I like you very much."

"So you didn't want to help Moses at first when he pressed himself on you because of this history of the girl?"

"Yes. You see Moses married Sarah Z. and they had a daughter, Miriam—who I've never met. Those who know Miriam say she is a wonderful girl."

"So what does Sarah Z. say about Moses' disappearance?"

I grimaced. "Not much, I'm afraid. You see, she died of brain cancer rather suddenly. It was over a decade ago."

"How terrible."

"Yes. It changed his life. It was around this time that Moses hooked up with Common Action. The rest is history."

"So he was a single parent raising a daughter."

"Yes."

"And he juggled this with a crusade for fair opportunity for others?"

"Yes."

"The man was a saint. Yet you still held this resentment against him?"

"I didn't know any of his personal history when he approached me. I've only discovered it since his disappearance."

"Since his disappearance?"

"Yes. He left me a journal of his life. I read it almost immediately. It has given me perspective on his life. It's a large part of the reason why I have agreed to carry his mantle."

"So when Moses approached you in the press conference, you were unaware that Sarah Z. was dead and all the other various details?"

"Correct."

"So basically, your relationship terminated when you came back from England and then instantly began again in front of the television cameras?"

"Essentially true. He did attend the same graduate school I did, The University of Chicago, but he quickly moved out of philosophy and into the law school. We had almost no contact."

"Were there any other surprises in the diary?"

"Only one: Josh Kaplan."

CHAPTER EIGHTEEN

Josh Kaplan

July 3, 2000

HE'S NOT GONE! I can't believe it. I've done everything that I could to ensure that Moses would be history. Somehow the man has nine lives. He escapes everything that I have tried to do. First, I decided to replace his legal team. The man responded by moving his people to a D.C. law firm, Cohen, Potts, and Sani. Moses was a sly one there. Sam and my other plants didn't even know what was happening. He thought that they were being let go and were commencing another career. At least that was what he told me. (And I believe Sam. After all, his daughter is going to college on a Common Action Scholarship—he wouldn't dare jeopardize that.)

But the staff wasn't really resumé shopping at all. They were being picked up by that buccaneer, Saul Sani. That renegade picked up the senior staff (the junior staff really did engage in a career change) with the intent of (as I know now) continuing the Humanity Hospital Case and promoting the Fair Opportunities Initiative as if it were their own!

Why, that has always been a Common Action project. It was there even before I became director. How dare they steal our idea!

Where I perhaps failed is in the instance of Peter Simon. This was Moses' link to Cohen, Potts, and Sani. My background people told me that Simon and Levi were definitely not pals. Sure they were in college together, but there were several documented fights between the two during the last three months. One occurred at Papa Giovani's Restaurant in which they came to blows. Peter struck Moses and bloodied his nose.

The police were called, but Moses did not press charges. He knew better. He knew that now he had a lever to get Simon to support him in his bid to move the case from Common Action to Cohen, Potts, and Sani. The little conniver.

All the time *I* thought that Moses was done. Remove the thermometer. Well roasted and well-done. But the guy was still maneuvering. What a selfish brute. I had won the war but he wasn't prepared to accept it. Bad loser.

Instead, he insinuates himself into an old college buddy and expects that he will just go and help him at the drop of a hat. Simon is way above Moses. The guy has a client list that is Blue Book all the way. He has no time for a guy in an 88 Toyota Corolla. So I guess Moses suckered the guy into a fight so that it was either 'support me on my project or I press charges.' How convenient. How calculated. How so like Moses.

Well, he won that one. He got me good. But I am not finished. I will strike quickly against Moses Levi. I must maintain control of this movement. At all costs, I am prepared to do anything. The man has been a thorn in my side for too long. It is time for this to stop. I will act and I will act decisively.

If Moses thinks that he has won this one, he is mistaken. It is time to ratchet the contest up a notch. And I am prepared to eliminate my foe.

CHAPTER NINETEEN

Peter Simon

July 15, 2000

8:00 ANTE MERIDIAN. Though Andrea and I had a two and a half hour dinner and another hour or so getting home, we started so early that it ended up being an early evening. I had been intent on telling Andrea virtually everything about the situation between Moses and me. I even told her that I was a suspect in Moses' murder investigation. This was not news to her. Andrea is a sharp lady. The only thing that has me confused is why she is interested in me. I mean if the situations were reversed, I wouldn't date a person like me—especially in this situation. It's one thing for a longtime friend or a spouse to stand by you and it's another for someone you have just met. (Though I will say that the intensity of our situations has probably accelerated things a pace.)

I noted that Saul's staff on Saturday morning was very light. Though Martin was there at his desk, I was relieved that not everyone worked his tail off every day of the week. I stopped by Saul's office, as was my custom before my meeting with the Duke. Saul was just about to leave.

"Already done for the day, Saul?"

"Hey, Peter, how are you?" Then Saul stopped. "Hey, look, Peter, I've got to talk to you. Do you have a second? Is that all right?"

What did he expect me to say? "Of course."

Saul brought me into the office and had me sit down. "Say, look, I loved your press conference on the evening news last night. Did you see it?"

"No," I said. "Do you have a tape?"

"Of course we do. The Duke will probably go over it with you."

"Great."

Saul took off his glasses. "Look, Peter. This criminal investigation is getting complicated. I'm not sure whether I can stop them from arresting you."

"Arresting me? I thought you said—"

Saul shook his head and then put his glasses back on. "I know, Peter. I understand totally where you're coming from. Believe me. It's just this Alice Minkas, you know. She's got the D.A.'s ear. Plus, there's the possibility that they'll go to the Federal Prosecutor."

"The Federal Prosecutor?"

"Yeah. On the theory that Moses Levi's civil rights were violated."

I sighed. "Okay. Where does that leave me?"

"Not good, Peter. There's a possibility that you will be arrested today."

"Today!" I thought about my date with Andrea. Of course the various prosecutors couldn't care less.

"I'm sorry to have to tell you this. But—"

"—Isn't there anything that you can do?"

"I'm afraid not, Peter. The way the system works is that unless there is new evidence that is brought to the fore, once a preponderance of evidence points in one direction, the prosecutor—whoever he or she is—is charged to act swiftly."

"But surely the evidence has not been exhausted. Isn't there anything else they can look at?"

"The grand jury has been busy as has the FBI unless you have some package from Moses that you are squirreling away somewhere," Saul said in a comical tone as he got up again, ready to exit.

Then it hit me. The journal! "Well, actually, Saul, there is one thing."

Saul smiled, expecting a joke as he made his way towards the door.

"Saul. I do have something. Moses sent me his personal journal. It was a second day Federal Express package. I received it July 5th."

Saul stopped. He was visibly shaken. "What did you say? A diary from Moses Levi? Why didn't you tell me sooner?"

"I don't know. I had to read it first. And then. I don't know. Things have been so hectic. At any rate, there is really not anything of value in it. I've read it over. Just short personal bits about his life since 1987."

Saul dropped his case and ran to me, grabbing my arms. "You mean that you have a thirteen-year personal journal from the man you are supposed to have murdered and you haven't told me?"

"It didn't occur to me."

Saul picked up his phone and gave Martin a message. In ten minutes we were at my house and I handed him the journal. Saul sat down at my oak 1930s Muskegon, Michigan kitchen table and he turned over the pages one at a time. He was skimming and grunting as he went through it. When he was finished, he looked back to me and nodded. Saul took off his glasses and smiled broadly. "Not bad. A hand-written journal. I'll have to review it carefully to see whether there's anything we can use, but it's sure to buy you some time—at any rate, Peter."

"Every day out of jail is blessing, I guess," I replied.

Saul packed up the journal in his briefcase. "I'll make you a copy of this, Peter, but for now, I've got some work to do."

I started to follow Saul to his car when he grabbed my shoulder and told me I was done for the day. I had no complaints. Might as well live it up while I can. Eat, drink, and be merry, for tomorrow you will die.

When Saul had left, I decided to call Andrea. Her line was busy. I didn't know who she was calling. An old boyfriend, perhaps? (Even worse, a current boyfriend?)

I decided to pick up a book that I had been meaning to read. After every five pages, I tried Andrea again. After thirty-five pages, still busy.

Another thirty-five did it. "Hi, it's Peter."

"Hi." Andrea's voice seemed peculiar to me.

"I was just calling to see whether you wanted to do anything today. It is Saturday and you had said we might do something?" I felt really queer about referring to any previous promise since I had importuned so often.

"Well yesterday put me back somewhat in my work, Peter. I don't think that today will work. I've got two meetings that I had scheduled that I have to do today and then there was one other meeting that I am just off to now." There was a pause.

I was very nervous. "How about tomorrow? I hear there's a Hitchcock festival at the National Film Institute tomorrow starting at one. We could meet at the Kennedy Center and watch until we drop. I know of a couple of places to eat in Foggy Bottom that aren't too expensive."

"Sounds good to me."

And that was that.

THE JOURNAL OF MOSES LEVI:
JUNE 4, 1996

My Miriam graduated from Walt Whitman High School. She has been accepted into Pembroke with a large grant. Both Sarah and I went to Pembroke. How nice it is for our daughter to follow after us.

THE JOURNAL OF MOSES LEVI:
JULY 5, 1996

Josh Kaplan was made the head of Common Action. He is such an ass. Really, I didn't much like his talk after he was made Director. I think he is inclined not to support much of the work I have been committed to. I don't know if this will be a problem or not.

THE JOURNAL OF MOSES LEVI:
SEPTEMBER 21, 1996

Miriam has taken a full load of science and math. Pembroke operates on the trimester system meaning that three courses is a full load. She's taking Introduction to Biology, Introduction to Chemistry, and Calculus. Math and science. I was a humanities guy. It's great that she's her own person but somehow I wanted her to enroll in a philosophy course.

THE JOURNAL OF MOSES LEVI:
JANUARY 5, 1997

Miriam did not do as well as she wanted to in her first semester. I told her that first of all the "pre-med" route is never easy. Second, she is at a top school. Pembroke is always rated among the six or seven best small colleges in the nation. When I went there, the top graduate in our class had a 3.55 grade point average and 3.2 was Phi Beta Kappa. This contrasted with many other schools in which an A was common and many achieved 4.0. I told her that it was different at Pembroke.

I also told her that they liked to weed out students in the introductory classes. It was some sort of sick rite of passage. "Let only the superior continue on" was their motto. The problem is that it is rather dubious whether they are really picking out the superior. They may have one particular mold and if you don't fit into it then they penalize you. This is not the superior; it is a principle of conformity. "Let only those who conform to our little model continue on." This should be the real motto. It is truly more accurate.

Anyway, I told her to persevere. Medical schools know that it is tough at Pembroke. They will take that into consideration. I wondered out loud to her whether a course in philosophy might give her a little perspective on her situation.

She's taking Biology 2, Chemistry 2, and Calculus 2. So much for a father's wisdom.

CHAPTER TWENTY

Miriam Levi

June, 1996

THIS MONTH I will graduate from Walt Whitman High School. I understand that they are holding the Commencement Ceremony at D.A.R. (Daughters of the American Revolution) Hall in Washington, D.C. Such a venue strikes me in a negative way on two counts. First, it is a structure that symbolizes the old Establishment in the nation. What could be more traditional than calling attention to one's Old Noble Blood? But Old Noble Blood is aristocratic and runs contrary to our traditional (all people count as one) attitude.

Second, there was an incident my father told me about in the Roosevelt Administration in which a black singer was not allowed to sing in the hall because she was black. I don't know much about the incident except that Eleanor intervened personally in the affair to find another venue, but it reminds me of the overt and ugly Anti-Semitism that my father tells me about from Grandpa Gert's time. Why do we honor the purveyors of bigotry?

At any rate, I'm graduating from high school and will attend Pembroke in the fall just like the parents. In so many ways, I wish that I could have known them then. How romantic to find the man you want to marry in college! I'm not sure things happen that way anymore. But their story is one that is emblazoned upon my mind: a talented philosophy student meets a talented English student at Dave's restaurant on a Sunday night because both wanted to avoid "mystery meat."

I wonder whether they still serve mystery meat on Sundays at Pembroke? I guess I'll find out.

I'm planning on being pre-med with an interest in going into medical research. I want to be the one who discovers a cure to cancer. Cancer took my mummy from me when I was ten. It was the great divide in my life. Every memory I have is stamped either mommy-time or after-mommy.

When you are ten you really can't understand that mummy is not coming back to you. People may tell you this. You may intellectually understand what the meaning of death is, but you don't really know what it means. At least I didn't.

Those first few months were filled with psychiatrist visits and group therapy. Then there is the sight of seeing your daddy just start crying in the middle of dinner. You're just sitting there eating and he bursts into uncontrollable tears. I had to be the one to comfort *him*.

But you know (thinking back on it) that maybe it wasn't so bad. It let me know that being torn apart inside at the loss of your mother wasn't unusual. I think in some ways that seeing my dad cry like he did in front of me actually opened me up. It let me confront some feelings of my own that I might not have. It was certainly better for me than those insipid support groups. I did not like strangers knowing my business. I even resented the psychiatrist (even though he was Jewish from the same Reformed Synagogue that we were starting to attend). I felt that he, too, was an outsider who might use what I said against me.

There was only my father (once my mother died). I love my daddy. I love him especially when I think of all he did for me—how he turned his life around for me. He used to be a big-time corporate lawyer at the most prestigious firm in Washington, D.C. The most prestigious law firm in the most prestigious city in the world. Yes, that was my father. It showed what he could do, if he wanted to. But when my mother died, he also changed his life around. He stopped practicing corporate law because it took too much time away from the family (me). If he were going to raise me properly, he needed lots of time. He needed time to be there for me when I needed him.

We created a daily routine. In the morning, Dad would wake up around 5:15 am and go out and get the paper, make his breakfast, read the paper, and then prepare my breakfast and my brown bag lunch for school. By this time, it was around 6:15 and he'd get me up and feed me while going over the last vestiges of homework or test preparation for that day. At 7:10 sharp we'd roll out and meet our respective days.

Since I lived only a mile from school, I'd walk home after school and study—doing everything I could until 6:00 when I'd start dinner. My dad generally rolled in around 6:30 at which time he took over dinner while we listened to the news on the radio.

After dinner, around 7:30, he'd do the dishes and the laundry while I folded and put away yesterday's laundry and prepared my list of questions I wanted to go over with him.

At 8:15 until bedtime (generally around ten o'clock) we'd go over our problem work in a very structured fashion. My dad used to say that unless I studied in a very structured way, I'd never be a success in school. He used to tell me stories about people he knew who stayed up all night studying—not because they were doing something fantastic, but because they were inefficiently applying themselves. He never wanted that for me: his pride and joy.

At ten, I would get ready for bed and call him when I was ready. I had a very small bedroom because our house had originally been designed as a "starter house" in the early 1950s when it had been constructed. There were three bedrooms, but only the master bedroom was normal-sized (meaning you could put a bed, a chest of drawers, a vanity and a couple bookcases in it).

Daddy would then read me something. It was generally rather short, like a story from an author my mother always admired, or a current event, or part of a brief that he was working on in court. Daddy always shared everything with me. Then he would put on some music for me to listen to while he went into the living room to read.

* * *

After about a year, Daddy stopped crying. It was then that he took another job. He started working for Common Action. I'm not sure why Daddy chose that job. It has only been a source of distress for him.

When he comes home after work he is often in a very foul mood. He needs some time by himself to readjust back to his real self. He doesn't talk about his work except in the most general ways (such as Joshua was very mean to him or was trying to make my father break the law). It's not easy. You'd think that working at a non-profit citizens' advocacy group would only attract the nicest people with the best intentions. Not true.

I worry about Daddy. Ever since he stopped crying, there was no consoling him. Daddy was a rock. At least that was what he wanted us all to believe. But I know better. I saw him when he was crying all the time. Now that he "had it all together" he was less all together than he was when he was crying.

Daddy grew to be a rather stiff and formal man. He would greet everyone in the same way: with a smile and a handshake—even me, his daughter! Moses Levi was not a hugger. I remember once when he took me to an Orioles game and I caught a foul ball. I was so ecstatic that I wanted to hug everyone in sight. I hugged my Daddy, Lori (the girl I brought as a guest to the game), and even the man in front of us who could have stopped me from catching the ball if he had wanted to. But Daddy did not hug me back. He allowed himself to be hugged, but would not hug me back in return. A shake of the hand—perhaps a slap on the back: that was Moses Levi's style.

It always hurt me that my father was so cold in this way, but I always attributed it to something that was connected to his new life, his life after my mummy.

Daddy never dated any other women. After Mummy, there was never anyone else. How could there be? Daddy is loyal and true.

* * *

Still, I sometimes dream about Mummy still being alive. I wonder what life would have been like with a mother to see me into my teenage years. Sometimes I create a vision of Mummy talking to me after school about life, science, and boys. I'm not so interested in boys, actually, because the boys at my high school are (for the most part) *very young and egocentric.*

But these are things that a girl likes to discuss with her mother. We could go to a coffee shop and nurse a cappuccino while we discussed the good, the true, and the beautiful.

Sure I can talk to Daddy, but there is something special about having a mummy.

*   *   *

Now I'm going to college (to Pembroke) just like my parents. I will study pre-med and go on to discover the cure to cancer and then my mummy will come back to life again and give me that half of my life that forever will be missing.

CHAPTER TWENTY-ONE

Andrea Warburton

July 15, 2000

5:30 ANTE MERIDIAN. I have gotten behind on my work. All this running around with Peter has put me back. I was very tired when I logged on to my computer and rambled through my files. I accidentally hit the 'archive' computer folder instead of the 'active' folder. Staring in front of me were the files for my mother and father. Without knowing why, I clicked into my father's file. My dad got Parkinson's disease when I was in my graduate program at Brown. The traditional treatments were not effective with him.

In the fall of 1993 I was faced with a choice. Either I could continue with my program and let my father deteriorate, or I could cut my program short by taking a master's degree and help him out as best I could. It was a rather difficult choice for me. On the one hand, I was a full adult with my own life and the opportunity to live it as I chose. On the other hand, my father was the person who saved my life over and over again as a child when I had severe asthma. He would sleep lightly each night and when I started gasping for air, he would come to me and administer the medicine and take my pulse in order that I might not go into cardiac arrest because of overdose.

On the times that I had to go to the hospital, it was my father who stayed in my room sleeping in a chair so that I wouldn't be alone. He monitored the medication and gave me the support that helped me survive.

Without my father, I would have died as a child. And now he was critically ill. How could I desert him?

I remember one phone call in which my mother told me how they had been shopping in the army PX (my dad was a disabled veteran of the Marine Corps in Vietnam). They were walking up and down the aisles when suddenly my father lost control of his locomotive ability. He was turning near the front of the grocery store when he suddenly started galloping forward—a fast, uncontrolled trot—into a display of canned goods. The display and my father toppled over.

Some privates viewed the episode. Did they offer to help my father to his feet? Did they sympathize with concern over what might have caused a fifty-three year old man to act so queerly? No. They laughed at him as if he were a drunk on skid row. One of the men—probably around nineteen or so—threw his empty orange juice carton at my father and hit him on the head. Hit him on the head! Laughed at him! The scum. Not fit to lick my father's shoe.

* * *

Most people with early onset Parkinson's disease can be treated effectively with the new dopamine derivatives. Not my father. He was doing poorly. My mother has never been very good around sick people. Her love gets in the way of effective action.

There was no one but me or my brother, Dave. But Dave's life was also difficult. He was still in college and not ready to shut things down for Dad.

* * *

It was more than I had counted on. After I took my master's in June of 1994, I moved back with my parents to help my dad. Unfortunately, this did not go as smoothly as I had hoped. There were more problems than merely my father's health. My parents' financial situation was a total mess. My mother hadn't worked since they got married and my father had to give up his job. He had been eligible for extended health benefits for eighteen months, but these had now run out--yet he was not old enough for Medicare. He could not get new insurance because who would take him? It was very difficult.

We were a family in need of money. It was at this time that I happened upon my first editing job. I met this person at the clinic where I took my dad, who worked with the Industrial Fasteners Newsletter (screw makers, for short). She told me about the freelance editing scene in the DC area.

One of the things going for you if you live in DC is that most professional organizations have a national headquarters. And most of them want to be in DC so that they can be close to the centers of power that can control their futures.

Each organization will hire a person to coordinate the various articles that will appear in their monthly, quarterly, semi-annual, or annual magazine. This person writes or assigns the articles and is also the production editor who makes sure that they come out right and on time.

Sometimes, these newsletter/magazines are really shills for key constituents—these are the bad jobs. Other times, they are honest attempts at representing what they are about to their members. These are the good jobs.

I began in this business in order to pay the bills and look after my father and mother. I eventually got to four quality jobs: 1. The National Medical Association (an association of African American physicians); 2. The Academy of Orthopedic Surgeons; 3. The National Guild of Hardware Dealers; and 4. The American Alliance of Alternative Energy. Each job paid me around fifteen to twenty thousand dollars a year (with the opportunity to make a little extra here and there). This allowed me to take care of my father.

On the downside, I was working eighty plus hours a week and hating every minute of it. No. That's not entirely correct. I enjoy interacting with real people (though I am a bit reserved by nature). I got to my final list through a process of trial and error. But just when I had achieved my perfect fit, my father died.

* * *

My mother followed my father within a year. Though she was a somewhat cantankerous woman, she loved very deeply.

That was sixteen months ago. Since then I have been involved in settling their almost non-existent estate. My parents' estate went into probate. It was awful. I took out some books from the library and represented the interests of myself and my brother. Since the estate was so small (under twenty thousand dollars), it was relatively easy, but it took time. Lots of time.

I split everything with Dave 50-50, but neither of us really cared. We are not a mercenary lot.

Then I went on autopilot.

*   *   *

When I met Peter at the concert, I must admit that I was surprised. Being a freelance editor, I must keep on top of the news. I had seen Peter's face on the news, but I did not immediately connect his face with the image from the screen. It is sometimes very hard to make the connection. When we sat in the pub and Peter started talking, I finally made the connection. I also knew that he was being talked about as a suspect in the Moses Levi murder. Why did I continue to see Peter if he might be a murderer? This is an interesting question. I am not sure whether I know the answer. It is true that I am desperate to change my life. Autopilot will only work so long. I half-wondered whether I should go back to school except that I have heard that the job market is terrible for teachers. I also enjoy some practical aspects of my work. What I hate is the hustling for jobs and the feeling that at any minute I may be unemployed and all alone.

Of course it is highly unlikely that I would lose all four of my jobs at once. It is also true that I don't need the income of all these jobs to live. When my father was sick, I lived at home. Since my parents' death, I moved to a small one-bedroom apartment with a low rent. I don't buy many clothes. I own a nine-year-old Toyota that I rarely drive and I eat moderately. Thus I can probably meet my economic requirements on one and a half of my jobs. The other two and a half just go into savings. I'd like to stop. But you can't really cut back. If I cut to two jobs and lost one, then I'd be out of luck. I suppose I could cut back to three, but I haven't really got the enthusiasm to turn out of autopilot.

If Peter were a murderer and decided to kill me, I'm not so sure that I wouldn't take it as a relief. Anything's better than what I have now. But that's not entirely true. I wouldn't really choose *anything*. For example, I wouldn't choose to be a drug dealer or to open a whorehouse. And actually, I never thought Peter was a murderer. The man may be arrogant (what man isn't), but he is not a killer. I could tell this almost immediately. Don't ask me how I know, but I do. For all Peter's bluster and posturing, he is actually an insecure person just like me looking for someone to commit with as much sincerity as he has. To protect himself from hurt he creates this "I don't need anyone" front. I know all about it. I invented it.

Peter has a need to be fed—not sexually (though I assume he is as capable as the next male), but emotionally. In this way, Peter has a good measure of what the Chinese call the yin. Those inclined toward the yin are not murderers.

Instead, Peter's yin balances his yang of law and philosophy. This is his real kinship with Moses. They both respected the law in a pure, juridical fashion. Peter believes in a sort of natural rights (which he won't admit to) but which is consistent with Moses' Judaism.

Judaism is Peter and Moses' common link. Though Peter styles himself as an atheist, he really isn't. Moses knew this, but Peter didn't. I know this and it draws me to the man.

*   *   *

I had to check a few facts for my editing jobs. I dialed-up onto the internet. As I waited for my connection, it again occurred to me I really hate what I'm doing. Let me back up a moment. I don't hate the little routines that I have established: creating the template for each issue, assigning stringers to write the stories, assembling it all together and supervising production. This is rather the same routine one would follow were she the editor for the National Association for Hardware Dealers or the editor for a literary novel. The mechanics are all the same. And if you believe in the written word, then there is a singular dignity to fulfilling these tasks in a diligent manner.

I remember Professor Dower at Brown saying, "Nihil est meilior quam vita diligissima." It is a necessary, true statement about the best life to lead, but it is incomplete. To say that nothing is better than the very industrious life, is to miss out on what you are industrious about. Surely, Nazis were very industrious about exterminating Jews! Thus, industriousness, by itself, is not enough. It must be directed toward a proper end.

Yet so much of my life since graduate school has been merely directed at industry. Diligence by itself is no virtue, even though sloth is generally a vice. It is properly-applied diligence that is the key.

But at that moment I failed in diligence. I decided all of a sudden to search the Web, not for information on the work I was supposed to do, but to the homepage of Peter's school, Notre Dame-Loyola. I began with a search of Peter. The results were not outstanding. Though he is one of the most published and prominent members of the faculty in academia at large, Peter was hardly mentioned in the internet descriptions.

On the way in and out of various screens, I saw an icon that said "University Communications." Without a thought, I double-clicked it. On the first page was a brief description of what University Communications was all about. In the lower right hand corner was a flashing hypertext link to IMMEDIATE JOB OPENINGS. I double clicked again.

EDITOR OF ALUMNI MAGAZINE. We are looking for a candidate who can write copy and coordinate a group of freelance writers for the magazine. The journal comes out monthly. Must have experience in magazine layout and design. Salary is competitive and includes benefits and tuition reimbursement. If you are interested, click for the online application.

Without another thought, I filled out the application and sent it along. What did it mean? Probably nothing.

Nothing is also what I had accomplished in the three-and-a-half-hours that I had been letting my fancy carry me. It was time for work. I found the site I needed for my research. By the time I logged off the internet it was ten o'clock. Almost immediately, Peter called.

"I can't keep our date. I'm way behind. Let's talk tomorrow."

"I hear there's a Hitchcock festival at the National Film Institute tomorrow starting at one. We could meet at the Kennedy Center and watch until we drop. I know a couple of places to eat in Foggy Bottom that aren't too expensive."

"Sounds good to me." And it did sound good. Peter sounded good. I'm almost afraid of this, yet I will not turn back. It is my destiny.

THE JOURNAL OF MOSES LEVI:
MARCH 17, 1997

The second term was better than the first. Miriam got an A in math and a B+ in both Biology and Chemistry. Next term she starts the macro-Biology sequence and is taking Physics 1 along with Statistics.

THE JOURNAL OF MOSES LEVI:
JUNE 15, 1997

The third term was off again. Miriam is sure she will never get into medical school at all. I try to comfort her, but she is taking it rather hard. In the fall she is taking Biology, Physics 2 and Philosophy!

THE JOURNAL OF MOSES LEVI:
SEPTEMBER 10, 1997

I thought that I had figured everything out on this. 2204 people contracted cancer that under normal circumstances would not have (according to statistical tables). Of these, 1502 died. It was now impossible to track them. My financial resources are increasingly limited. I live in a house, but that is a relic of the old life. Perhaps when Miriam is on her own I will sell the house and try to contact those I have harmed. There should be some way I can do this on the internet. I just don't know how.

THE JOURNAL OF MOSES LEVI:
SEPTEMBER 21, 1997

It occurred to me that perhaps the reason my Miriam is so stressed out is that she is trying to please me. They say that it is natural for daughters to want to please their fathers—especially in cases in which the mother is dead. Have I really told Miriam how proud I am of her? Are words enough? There is a Common Action event in November near the Twin Cities. I could visit Miriam and let her know that she need do nothing to win my love. She has it without asking.

Is this a legitimate concern or am I just paranoid?

THE JOURNAL OF MOSES LEVI:
FEBRUARY 18, 1998

I couldn't do November, but I did visit Miriam last weekend. I don't know if it's global warming or not, but I remember Pembroke winters as much colder and with more snow than I saw.

Miriam is taking some Core distribution requirements this term and only one science course. She should finish the macro sequence this year and move into the micro sequence. We had a spaghetti supper at a little bistro in town. I told her that I had taken her mother to this same place (it was called Dave's then and only served pizza). I had originally found out about the place from Peter when he had a job delivering pizzas to the town, Pembroke and St. Olaf's on the hill. Peter always said that Pembroke students were lousy tippers. 'Really it is Pem-I'm-broke, therefore no tippy for you.'

Anyway, when Peter went away to England, I started dating Sarah. And she really liked going to Dave's because instead of cutting pizza into huge "pie shaped" pieces, they cut it into a number of rectangles, each of which was very small. You could put one into your mouth and eat it in a bite without having to worry about the limp crust dripping oil and cheese all over your pants.

We had a good time. I feel that my daughter is now becoming an adult friend.

THE JOURNAL OF MOSES LEVI:
JUNE 15, 1998

Miriam wants me to advise her on whether she should change majors. She got another so-so report card on her science class. She got an A- and a B+ in her core classes of English and Government. Maybe she should follow in her father's footsteps and be a humanities chap.

Miriam wonders whether G-d is calling her elsewhere. "You know, Dad, it isn't as if there is a megaphone with a burning bush and all that! You have to face reality. Maybe, I'm not just meant to be medical researcher."

What am I to say to her? Me who went toward philosophy and then backed into law. Who gave me advice? Would I have even accepted advice? No way. Should I have even accepted advice? Ah, if I had then perhaps I could have avoided. . .

What I said to her was, "You have to handle this one on your own, Miriam. I can't help you."

"You can't or you won't?"

"Because I can't, I won't. If I could, I would. But at some point there is responsibility. Responsibility and autonomy are two banks that border the path toward personhood. You must be autonomous or else you are a slave. But accompanying this autonomy is responsibility."

We sat staring at each other.

Finally, she asked me, *"Given that I've taken intro to philosophy, what other two courses would you recommend in philosophy?"*

"Anything that gets you reading Plato, Aristotle, Kant or Hegel sound pretty good to me."

"Were any of them scientists?"

"Aristotle invented the discipline of biology."

Miriam didn't answer, but her jaw dropped two inches.

CHAPTER TWENTY-TWO

Miriam Levi

December 28, 1997

I JUST GOT my first term grades from Pembroke. They were terrible. I got a B+ in Biology, a B in Chemistry, and a C+ in Calculus. I really don't understand this. I got such good grades in high school and I was supposed to be going to one of the best public high schools in the country, Walt Whitman.

I followed my father's advice on creating very structured study sessions and always going to bed early. I followed the routine down to the letter. But look what I have to show for it. Nada.

When my report card came in the mail (around December 23rd) I didn't show it to my dad. How could I? I knew he wouldn't yell or anything. It's not like that. That isn't him. But I knew he'd be disappointed. I mean, *I* was disappointed. If he said that he *wasn't* disappointed, then I'd know that he was either saying that for my benefit (probably the case) or he simply didn't care.

I knew he cared. When I finally showed him my report card, yesterday, he acted as if everything was fine. "This doesn't mean anything," he said. "The medical schools know about Pembroke. The grades there are very rough—even compared to other highly selective colleges and universities. You must remember that there is this insane notion that in math and science there must be a ritual "weeding out" process in which the weaker and less qualified people will be discovered and summarily dismissed from their profession. This is absurd on several counts, not the least of which is that it promotes only those who mirror the practitioners of the time. There is no incentive for mavericks.

There is no incentive to hire the disenfranchised of society. This is why medicine has been dominated by white males for so long.

"When good people fail in science, it is an indictment of the discipline as much as it is an evaluation of novice inquirers."

I loved my father's words. I wonder whether he was saying this because it was true or because he wanted to keep my spirits high. There is no way to know. My father is capable to acting in either way. He has a passion for truth, but he is also the most loyal person I've ever met. No one's trust is lost in his hands.

THE JOURNAL OF MOSES LEVI: SEPTEMBER 21, 1998

This son-of-a bitch Josh Kaplan is trying to take over my Fair Start project. I know that Common Action has garnered tons of money under his tenure, so that my making a scene about this will only bring about my demise. I care only about the proper fulfillment of my vision. If I can help America achieve racial, gender, religious, and sexual-orientation equality, then I will have brought our Democracy into the Promised Land of Human Freedom and Personal Fulfillment. It is what I live for.

But this Administration (Democrats who act like Republicans) will not help me in any way. I need the organization to further my mission. How can I work with a man who is itching for total control? This is a man who is "on the right side" but for all the wrong reasons. I do believe that the "right reasons" are critically important. Motivation is crucial. Over and over again it is upheld by many writers in the Wisdom Literature. Action is obviously most important, but without proper motivation, it can become accidental.

What am I to do? Should I knuckle under to Josh Kaplan? Should I resign and live on my retirement plan?

Somehow I know that I cannot quit. My history with Waste Disposal, Inc. had constrained me. I have done so much harm that I cannot turn away. I have no choice. I am the single man who is driven to redeem himself and his generation from all their harmful and selfish actions.

I really have no choice. It is not a path I want to choose. I would rather make myself a total devotee of my daughter, Miriam. But I know that she understands. She knows that I do this for her as well as for me.

Sometimes you have to act in one way even though you know that the result will probably be self-destruction. I have enemies. I know it. What I must do is to enlist others to take up the cause in case my enemies prove successful.

THE JOURNAL OF MOSES LEVI: NOVEMBER 8, 1998

Miriam told me that I have pushed and manipulated her into taking a biology/pre-med major and that she has been a total failure. Her grades are not nearly good enough to get into even the worst medical school. She told me that it would have been better that she had never been born and that I was a domineering and manipulative father.

Perhaps she's right that I have been a poor father, but I cannot agree to the stuff about it being better that she had never been born. I don't think of her as a failure, but I seem incapable of conveying my esteem of her to her. I admire her greatly. I love her and couldn't be more proud of her and her work ethic. She did not go to college expecting to have one long party. She went on a mission seeking to become a biomedical researcher who would find a cure to the sort of cancer that killed her mother. She has kept to the path and has done her best. I have tried to encourage her in the most honest ways that I can.

Who knows if she really has what it takes to get accepted to medical school and then to become a biomedical researcher who can eventually run a lab following her strategies? I want to support the dream, yet I do not want to be someone who blindly pushes her down a path that will lead to failure.

Miriam gets better grades in humanities courses than she does in science courses. Does this mean that she should really be trying humanities? After all, that's what I did. But that's the whole point. I am reluctant to make that point because it seems as if I am trying to make her into a little clone of me.

Sarah Z. also chose humanities. Maybe it's in her blood. But I would never—under any circumstances—play the card of her dead mother.

How can I guide my daughter without dominating her? Is showing her love letting her possibly go in the wrong direction, or is it to enter into a dialogue with her about science? Yet, I feel that there are so many strikes against women in science—even today—that I am reluctant to say anything. But is this, again, just another ego trip on my behalf? Do I want to show the world that I have a daughter who has made it in a man's world? Is this a part of my liberalism? Another way to show off to my peers?

This gets so complicated.

THE JOURNAL OF MOSES LEVI: MARCH 15, 1999

Miriam got her MCAT scores back. She made the 98th percentile overall. I decided to send her a big basket of Harry and David fruit with a note of congratulations.

THE JOURNAL OF MOSES LEVI: MAY 6, 1999

Miriam was accepted as a paid intern at the National Institutes of Health. She will be working in a lab that is studying cancer. They say that the three factors that affect admission to medical school are: 1. Grades as an undergraduate in science courses, 2. MCAT scores, and 3. Recommendations from teachers and those in the field. With this job, Miriam has a chance at two of these three opportunities.

CHAPTER TWENTY-THREE

THE JOURNAL OF MOSES LEVI:
SEPTEMBER 21, 1999

I have set up a home page on the internet for those who care to click on to it. My home page describes how sorry I am for the wrong that I perpetrated in my defense of a company I believed to be guilty but had been found innocent in a court of law.

I tried not to write anything that would be libelous, because I repeated over and over how Waste Disposal had been found innocent. But I also made it clear that the American Legal System is one that is not very good at seeking Truth. We make it a contest. We assume that our all-mighty idol, Competition, would take care of everything. In fair Competition, all will work out fine. Vested interests dissolve as the pure energy of self-interest drives the contestants toward their pure, procedural goal: the conviction of the party with the poorer lawyer and the acquittal of the party with the superior lawyer. What a system!

Here is a short representative sample of the replies I received:

Thomas Aquinas said that it was better to do a deed with a good intention than with an ill intention. If the actions that we commit turn out to be flawed, then at least you know that you acted in good faith. What more can we demand of anyone?

If you were a part of the plot that robbed me of my mother and then covered it up, then I must tell you that I cannot and will not forgive you. Kinda late in the day for that? Don't you think?

Our family broke up due to the resettlement. No one died, but our lives were ruined. You should be sent to prison.

I am going to try to find out where you live. I'll tell you what you deserve, and that's a bullet in your skull.

I'm not a part of that group or nothing. But I clicked onto your Web site and I thought it was totally perverted. You old farts really think you can find forgiveness in cyberspace? Click onto Aryan Nation.com for some real low down on true revenge.

Thank you for your note. I lost my husband to cancer. I know that you changed your life, and I forgive you.

How easy do you think it is to assuage your conscience? A web site doesn't do it, buster.

I would like to forgive you. But I cannot lie. You and your rich buddies screwed my life and my brother. We were both rendered sterile by your lousy chemicals and as a result we could not raise a family. My husband divorced me because of it. I am a Muslim and in my community I became damaged goods. My brother, when he realized that he was sterile, went out in his car and tried to kill himself. What he succeeded in doing was smashing into another car and killing the mother, father and one of the two children. My brother now navigates through life in a wheelchair. What a tragedy that through no fault of my own my life and that of my brother have been so damaged. I would like to forgive you because I believe in the basic concept of forgiveness. But I cannot honestly do so.

Rot in hell you goddamn Jewish bastard.

CHAPTER TWENTY-FOUR

Andrea Warburton

September 21, 2000

9:00 ANTE MERIDIAN. I logged onto my computer while I finished my café latte that I bought on the way to Notre Dame-Loyola. I have only been on the job for six weeks, but already I feel at home. This was the first-full time permanent job I had ever held. Everything else had been summer work, college work contracts, or my freelance hustling on the trade journal marketplace. There is something very satisfying about the thought that if I get sick or disabled for an extended period of time that my income will not disappear. It must be the feeling that Dave has working for the Government. A small school is not as secure as the government, but after all, we *do* have a hundred million-dollar endowment whose annual interest pays for 1/5th of the annual operating costs. Another fifth is covered by government grants while yet another fifth is funded by a restricted scholarship endowment. That means that 60% of all expenses are covered before a single student puts down her tuition! I know that at Pembroke and Brown those figures approach 100%, but 60% affords a pretty good margin for error.

For the first two weeks on the job I kept all my other jobs, but then everything seemed so right that by the middle of the third week I dropped the American Alliance of Alternative Energy (they were my least favorite anyway).

Then I waited another month. The next on the block was the National Guild of Hardware Dealers. I never liked Jamie who acted like she owned the home office in Chicago. She treated the DC contingent as lobbyist animals who were all on the take.

Now I am back to my two stable journals, the National Medical Association and the Academy of Orthopedic Surgeons. I will try to stay with them for a while until I know for sure that I want this job. There is little doubt in my mind now, but I do know things can change.

Another interesting plus about my job is that I can teach a class in the English Department starting in the spring semester. I will be an adjunct member of the department and can go to department meetings and the like. This will let me know whether I really want to continue my education and get my Ph.D. If I do, the university will cover the cost of my tuition at George Washington University, The University of Maryland, American University, or The Catholic University of America (the Ph.D. granting institutions in the area in English).

Suddenly, I feel that I am almost out of the deep tunnel in which I had been resting on autopilot. Once I start teaching I will give up at least one of the other journals. (I am ethically committed to the cause of African American physicians so that it might be impossible for me to detach from the National Medical Association.) At any rate, I have never felt so good about working.

*   *   *

My phone rang. It was Peter. "Are we on for lunch today?"

"Sure. At noon?"

"I'll come by."

Peter has been so much happier since the shadow has moved away from him. He's on the television occasionally in his role as public spokesman for Fair Opportunity. I believe that he has grown into the role. Generally, I accompany him on out-of-town trips. I appreciate Peter's reserve that allows *me* to set the pace for our relationship. When I feel the time is right, I will ask Peter to marry me. Near side, it might be six months. Far side, it might be twelve months. Beyond that, he's toast.

A call comes in. It is another alumnus who wants to respond to the query I sent out on the ND-L experience. This will be the lead article in our November issue and will coincide with our annual fundraising campaign. If I get out the vote, I will be a candidate for Director of this unit. I am already over-qualified. But I don't care. The pace of this work soothes me. I have emerged from the tunnel to face the world.

THE JOURNAL OF MOSES LEVI:
MARCH 15, 2000

Josh Kaplan phoned me today that he is taking my staff away immediately. He was really upset about the Time Magazine and the Newsweek Magazine articles about the Humanity Hospital Case and my associated Fair Opportunity Initiative. The man is really very controlling. He has a management style that insists on getting into the details of everyone in the organization. This can only work in a small community such as Common Action. All the prominent business schools eschew the micromanagement style. Josh doesn't really get it.

Josh is basically a good guy (I think) except that he is the classic over achiever. His reach exceeds his grasp. But fortunately for me, he is somewhat incompetent. I think I can keep one step ahead of this guy. Sometimes he frightens me. Is evil really banal? If so, then . . .

What Josh wants to do is to replace my staff man-by-man with his own people. These traitors are led by Sam Rodriguez (his main plant). I am so thankful that Josh is so incompetent. I can feed Sam information (or rather misinformation) to throw him off.

But this move to eliminate my staff is real. I must think of some way to counteract it.

THE JOURNAL OF MOSES LEVI:
MARCH 18, 2000

It just came to me. Peter Simon. My old college roommate. I read in the Washington Business Journal that he has been doing some consulting with the Fortune Five Hundred companies who are in the area and that he has a lucrative contract with Cohen, Potts, and Sani. They are a "swing firm" meaning that they do corporate law and rake in the bucks, but they also do a hefty share of pro-bono work. These are the guys that I must get to support me so that Common Action's pullout will not mean the end of my journey. I will have to contact Peter immediately.

THE JOURNAL OF MOSES LEVI:
MARCH 19, 2000

When I called Peter at 11am he went into a fit. He didn't like being called on a Sunday morning and he didn't much like talking to me. Old ghosts, perhaps. However, I got the wedge in. I think there is promise here.

THE JOURNAL OF MOSES LEVI:
MARCH 23, 2000

Peter finally got back to me after a dozen more calls. He gave me a name and agreed to come to a news conference tomorrow. I need Peter.

THE JOURNAL OF MOSES LEVI:
MARCH 24, 2000

I had to pressure Peter at the news conference. And I know that he was a bit upset with me at a lunch afterwards. He took a punch at me. Same old Peter. I know he'll come through.

THE JOURNAL OF MOSES LEVI:
MARCH 27, 2000

Peter has agreed to meet with me with Saul Sani tomorrow. This may be the break I have been waiting for.

THE JOURNAL OF MOSES LEVI:
MARCH 28, 2000

Peter came through. Saul Sani has agreed to pay the salaries of Ulanda Washington, Jane Eliot, Sam Rodriguez, and Ayanna Smith for a limited time until I can get a new sponsoring agency. This is rather decent of the guy. I am very thankful to Peter, though he still is unresponsive to me. At least his actions show he's on my side.

THE JOURNAL OF MOSES LEVI:
APRIL 10, 2000

Miriam has been accepted to Johns Hopkins Medical School! Her grades weren't the highest, but all things considered, she made it. Maybe she's on the right road after all.

CHAPTER TWENTY-FIVE

Miriam Levi

June 30, 2000

I've just graduated from Pembroke (June 17th). It was a wonderful day. Daddy came with his camera loaded with film. He took all thirty-five pictures in two days. I've never seen my father so wasteful as he was taking all those pictures.

"You'll want these for posterity," he said as he snapped one more angle of me holding my diploma.

Daddy stayed in the College Inn, a motel just outside of town. I stayed in the dorm so that I could soak up the atmosphere for just one more day. We had dinner at Dave's (just like he did with Mummy). Daddy declared that the old place hadn't changed at all, but I find that hard to believe. Anyway, we shared a large pepperoni pizza and a pitcher of coke. Daddy said he had beer in the old days, but I don't drink.

It was a grand evening. After dinner, Daddy accompanied Margaret and me to a concert at the Music and Arts Center. Then I hung out with some friends while Daddy went to the motel to make some business calls.

The next day I marched. It was so exciting. President Clinton delivered his last Commencement Address of his Presidency. The sky was blue. I got the right diploma. I didn't trip and there were no embarrassing incidents that you often hear about at college Commencement Ceremonies.

Life was very good that day. In fact, life has been very good since I heard that I have been accepted for medical school at Johns Hopkins. This made me ecstatic. My grades were only around a 3.3, but I did well on my MCATS, and I had some good recommendations. I had been so sure that my gamble on getting admitted to medical school (especially a prestigious one) was in vain. I have made so many phone calls to Daddy venting my frustration. He was a rock. He encouraged me to continue. He never had any doubt in me. For that I am thankful. Without his confidence in me, I'm not sure I would have made it.

The only note of disappointment on the day was that unlike my mother, Sarah Z, I would not be getting married soon after graduation. I did not meet the man of my dreams at Pembroke. It didn't happen. In fact, almost all of my dates were of the "friends hanging with friends" variety. Perhaps I'm too fat. My father doesn't think so, but what is he supposed to say? Miriam, you're getting pudgy, my dear.

No. His role has always been to support me. The man is almost incapable of criticizing me at all. I'm his little princess. The only family he has left in the world. What is he supposed to say?

But I am fat. I'm 5' 10" and one hundred and twenty-five pounds. I do no sports, but I swim recreationally and lift weights at the gym. I wish my Daddy would come right out and tell me I'm fat so that I might undergo a crash diet that would make me better.

*   *   *

Aside from my weight problem, I've nothing to complain about. Well, perhaps one thing: my dad's job. He hasn't taken a salary from this job for a long time (lucky thing for me that Pembroke provides 100% of demonstrated financial need for its students), but still his boss, Josh, has been on his case. The man hates my father because my father is good, honest, and hardworking: everything Josh isn't.

Well, lately, we've been getting these terrible phone calls. They run something like this. Ring Ring Ring. "Yes, hello?"

"Moses. Moses. You're history, Moses. Understand?"

"Who are you? Why are you calling?"

"You're history." Click. Dial tone.

Or this one: "Yes, hello?"

"Your time's up, Moses."

Or this one: "Count the hours. The end is near."

I tried hitting *69 on my phone. It didn't work. I called the phone company. They said that there had been no phone call during that interval. I called the police who contacted the phone company and decided that I was a nut case.

I knew that my father was working on a public interest case on his Fair Opportunity Initiative. He's been on that case for years, but in the last six months several of the major newspapers and the popular news magazines have featured stories about my dad. The Fair Opportunity Initiative is a lightning rod. People either revere my father for the work he is doing for equal opportunity or they hate him for it.

The Justice Department was not inclined to get involved in investigating these phone calls since the Administration is rather "middle-of-the-road" on such issues and it's an election year. And though they might admire my father's spirit, they are *not* inclined to do anything about it.

Well, I tell you, I'm apprehensive. I read a novel about Martin Luther King, Jr. entitled *Dreamer,* in which people ignored death threats against Dr. King. It went on for several years until an assassin's bullet ended the life of one of the saints of the Twentieth Century. Was this what was happening to my father?

Since I am not working this summer (a sort of post-graduation "fling" to live at home and not go work as a galley slave at a lab at the National Institutes of Health, as I had since high school), I have some free time. I decided to visit the Rabbi, Moshe BenDavid, at our synagogue. I sat in one of the simple Shaker-styled wood chairs that adorned his rather spartan office.

"Have you tried using that new trick that the phone company has of hitting the star key and then punching in the numbers six and nine?" Rabbi BenDavid was a middle-aged man about my father's age. He went to school at the University of California, Berkeley, and got a master's degree in Religious Studies before going to seminary at the Graduate Theological Union also at Berkeley. We were sitting in his office. It was a room that was made out of basic cement blocks that had been painted off-white. He had a rather simple bookcase with about five hundred titles of volumes that he had read or intended to read. On the floor was a carpet from Israel. Not many people know that there is still a small active weaving guild in the Holy Land that makes hand-made carpets of a quality similar to those of their Islamic brothers. I knew, from an earlier part of my life, that each knot on the rug had been dedicated to a psalm of David. His desk was also very simple. There was little ornamentation in Rabbi BenDavid's office.

I outlined everything that I had done. This really impressed the Rabbi.

"You know, I've always felt your father was a man of G-d. Do you understand what I mean by that?"

I nodded.

"No, you don't." Rabbi BenDavid began pulling at his close-cut graying beard. "You see, The Master of the Universe often has devices we don't understand. Why, there are some of his prophets that he has so honored that he has assumed them into heaven without going through the process of death."

"I don't understand. How can you go to heaven without dying? Besides, isn't life after death a controversial doctrine?"

"I let the controversies be carried out by the Talmudic scholars. I am merely a humble servant of G-d. All I can tell you is the world the way I see it. You don't have to agree with me. But remember, it was you who sought me out."

"Of course, Rabbi BenDavid. I didn't mean to be rude. I just don't understand what it means to be assumed into heaven."

"Neither does anyone else. It is a mystery. I think that those who seek the company of the Master of the Universe must be prepared. He has many tricks up his sleeve. I wouldn't put anything past Him."

"But these death threats—"

"As a good daughter you must do everything that you can in response to them. You must hit the star, six, and nine. You must call the phone company, you must call the police. You must tell your father. You must try the Justice Department and the FBI. But you've done it all. Your father is leading a crusade. He is fighting for liberation for many Americans. This has always been an essential mission for Jews— especially in this epoch of history.

"When you have done what you must do—according to your duty— then you have to let go. Ultimately, there is much beyond our control. For all power resides in the Master of the Universe." Rabbi BenDavid then put his hands to his face as if he were feeling some great emotion. It only lasted a moment.

"It is all out of our hands, Miriam. Yours and mine. We must trust that your father is part of a larger plan than either you or I can understand. Until the Messiah comes, everything in life is still a mystery. Our lot as Jews is to be strong. We must endure. There will be no one who will bring us salvation but ourselves in relation to G-d.

"Your father is a great man. I'm sure you know that. Great things happen to great people. You and I will have to sit on the sideline on this one and await the outcome."

THE JOURNAL OF MOSES LEVI:
JUNE 2, 2000

Time is running out for another sponsor. Saul Sani will not be able to bank roll us forever.

THE JOURNAL OF MOSES LEVI:
JUNE 5, 2000

Josh is turning up the heat. Everything I say or do he reacts to. Maybe I should fire my staff, except for Ulanda.

THE JOURNAL OF MOSES LEVI:
JUNE 6, 2000

My sojourn on the Web was a failure. There is really no way to create a spirit of forgiveness in the general sense. What does this mean?

It means that forgiveness is an interpersonal action that individuals must solicit from each other. It means that there is perhaps a proper scope of life in which one interacts with one person at a time. This means that one must pay heed to the level of his prominence because the consequences multiply all too quickly.

It also means that even though the model is incomplete, that we should, nevertheless, try to solicit the forgiveness—individually—of those we have harmed. After all, we harmed them individually. Why shouldn't their individual human dignity manifest itself in the process of forgiveness? The model as presented is correct.

What is there for me to do in these circumstances?

THE JOURNAL OF MOSES LEVI:
JUNE 13, 2000.

I think Peter will never be with me as he once was.

THE JOURNAL OF MOSES LEVI:
JUNE 17, 2000

My Miriam graduated from college! President Bill Clinton spoke at her Commencement Ceremonies. What a thrill. I know that I was excited at her graduation from high school, too, but it did not compare to this. College. Such a difference. Such a struggle. My Miriam made it! Afterwards, we went out to the spaghetti restaurant and celebrated.

"You know, they used to call this place 'Dave's' when I went to Pembroke. I took your mother here when we started dating," I said.

"Yes, Daddy. I know. You've told me about this a hundred times."

"You've heard the story?"

"Yes, but that doesn't mean that I don't want to hear it one more time."

CHAPTER TWENTY-SIX

Saul Sani

October 2, 2000

> *Waves lapping the pebbled shore;*
> *Some promising swells, dissolve—*
> *Others suddenly arise and thunder,*
> *Stretching beyond all others,*
> *Before they, too, retreat and slide away.*

THIS POEM IS ATTACHED to a little plaque that I have propped against my lamp. I read it countless times every day. Over time I draw different meanings from it. I understand that it is a translation from a Japanese poet who wrote in the so-called double form from the seventeenth century. Instead of the 5-7-5 Haiku form or the 7-5-7-5-5, they employ 7-7-10-7-10. Each "10" is a double 5, hence the title "double form."

Unlike other Japanese poetic forms in which a theme is given and fixed into a concrete description of a natural event, the double form makes you guess the theme. This is more like the hidden rocks in the sand garden in which the audience must guess or speculate upon the positioning of hidden rocks and/or the fullness of partially revealed stones. It is up to the observer to ferret out the meaning.

When I think of my practice as an attorney, I know that so much that is promising turns out to be nothing at all. It is the way of the world. When I think of the same thought from my own perspective on vacation, it also holds true. The reason I really enjoy vacationing on beaches is that the waves are so regular and irregular at the same time. When you position yourself in a low beach chair atop your grass mat and under your umbrella, you can become fixated on the continuous rhythm of it all. The sounds of the waves display a commonness, but also reveal a subtle variety as each wave breaks. Similarly, the smell of the water (whose nuance changes daily and even on each tide), and the tastes as the spray reaches your tongue (I always sit as close as I can), you experience a mildly vacillating saline experience. Even the touch of the brine spray upon the skin can sometimes be oily and sometimes simply drying. And of course the greatest variety of all is in the sight of the waves as they approach. No two waves are identical.

This experience is heightened as one enters the water and lets the force of the water carry him to shore. Generally this is called body surfing. Anyone who has tried it will attest that the experience is one of constant variation. No two waves are really alike. One walks out into the water until it is just below the armpits. Then you look up and face your future. One doesn't want to commit to every wave. Some look promising from afar and turn out to be nothing. Others just come up on you. If you are nimble, you can catch them nonetheless. Those are the waves that deliver the most pleasure.

My son Samuel liked to ride the waves with me when he was growing up. His mother, may she rest in peace, was our most ardent spectator. We would be out for hours. It was paradise.

But it is also true that even the best of waves retire and pass away when they have done what they were able to do. It is that finality that gives an intensity to the entire endeavor.

So now I surround myself with reminders of the ocean and beaches. And twice a year I try to travel to a beach for a personal vacation. Right now I am considering a brochure from Bora-Bora. They offer an attractive package. I'm too busy for a voyage, but this air-hotel package is really attractive. I might ask Matthew to scan the internet travel sites in order to determine how good this plan really is.

Bora Bora sounds very exotic to me. I wonder what sort of beaches they have. I have heard that their beaches have coral close in. If so, then I'd have to remain a spectator on my low beach chair and mat. But that's okay, too.

Another thing that strikes me about the waves is that they do not stop. So often people have the image that in life they can "make-it" and then it's over. This is not the model of the waves. The waves are continuous. Life is continuous. Business is never static: if you are not moving forward, then you are declining. There is no such thing as achieving some status that confers non-temporal, eternal value. This ideal is reserved for G-d.

Over the past few months, since Peter Simon approached me about helping out Moses Levi, I have moved forward. I must admit that at first we were rather reticent at making this commitment. One important factor was that we had begun using Peter Simon with many of our important clients as a consultant for their businesses. In our current climate, there is a real market for focused ethical advice. This fits in squarely with our strategic marketing plan. We knew that Moses Levi was very high profile, but was also a man who had alienated almost everyone of power and substance that he knew.

Moses was going down, so he reached for the last and only chance he had: Peter Simon.

This was not bad for us. If we went forward with Peter being prominently displayed, his market value would increase. It is not exactly true that all publicity is good publicity, but muddied publicity (that is later corrected) is just fine. The fact that Peter seemed to be reluctant and then was subsequently a prime suspect in Moses' murder was not decisive. What counted most was Peter's obvious ambivalence. He was not out and out rejecting Moses. He was torn. This matched the country's own ambivalence toward Affirmative Action (and other tough ethical dilemmas).

In a real sense, Peter's inner struggle was an even more credible spokesperson for the cause than he would have been if he had embraced it initially full speed ahead. This is because most people when confronted with an ethical conundrum in their business or personal life are ambivalent. Thus, the common man and woman were able to identify with Peter Simon in a way that they could not identify with had Peter been a zealot. He is like them, and they know it.

The only problem is that Peter doesn't know it. Like most academics, he suffers from a delusional sense of superiority to ordinary people. But Peter's personal difficulties with Moses made these airs vanish to the viewing public. Then, when Peter felt the pressure of a murder investigation, he moved to his best behavior. That was all that was necessary to endear him to the hearts of millions.

He became Moses' man--plus. In many ways he's a better spokesman than Moses was. And with Moses dead or missing, Peter's image is clear and positive.

I have Peter under a personal services contract for five years with an option for five more. Peter's worth to our firm has increased a hundred fold since this episode began. It was almost perfectly scripted from our point of view. Here we have a consultant who is very good (but rather difficult to work with) who undergoes a personal transformation that includes dropping his academic hauteur, discovering a voice that resonates with the people, and finding a second wife—all in one! The man has been transformed.

And that's not all. Peter's odyssey brought me into contact with Syd Pawalchowski. Syd's career with Omnium Ltd. is legendary. He is the best of the best—so much so that he is nick named The Duke of Omnium.

Omnium Ltd. represents clients (generally multi-national corporations and even nations themselves) in order to close a deal, get legislation passed, or move to instigate a war by a major power. They are one of the most influential and powerful institutions in the world. However, it is their mode of operations that they always work in secret. They are effective because few people really know of their existence. There are a number of "results oriented" firms in the world, but none with a client list like Omnium.

Part of the whole aura of Omnium is that it is rather difficult to approach them about doing work for you. They do not solicit business. They do not speak with people they do not know very well. In other words, it is almost impossible to become a client of Omnium.

When Peter asked me to bankroll Moses' project, I wanted to talk to their chief litigator, Ulanda Washington. Ulanda and I had a very long meeting in March about the entire Humanity Hospitals case. Ulanda was very frustrated in the case. This is because she saw a way to bring the case to a close with a settlement. The case began when Humanity Hospitals, Inc. (one of the largest for-profit managed healthcare plans in the country) decided to eliminate its Affirmative Action policies. Now Humanity Hospitals, Inc. was bound by Federal regulations because it received tons of money from Medicaid and Medicare. Humanity Hospitals was pushing the envelope. They saw deteriorating support for Affirmative Action around the country and they wanted to save money by cutting red tape.

What Ulanda had done was to negotiate some policy changes that resembled the Fair Opportunity Initiative in return for a waiver of any fine or punitive actions against the hospital network. But Moses felt that without punishment, there could be no redemption. So Moses held out against the settlement.

At the same time, Ulanda was working on a big case for the Mexican Trucking Consortium that was suing Nineball Express (the largest U.S. Trucking Company) under the terms of NAFTA (the North American Free Trade Agreement). Under the agreement, Mexican Trucking firms could come into the United States and deliver goods produced in Mexico directly to their destinations (instead of the previous practice of having to unload at the border and having their loads transferred to trucks run by Nineball Express). This difference was worth hundreds of millions of dollars in lost revenue.

Ulanda had taken on the case after Moses had been directly contacted by the Mexican Ambassador. Ulanda believed in the case and would only agree to continue to be a part of Moses' team under my sponsorship if I agreed to press for her settlement offer in the Humanity Hospitals case and if I agreed to help her with the Mexican Trucking Consortium against Nineball Express.

I agreed. It was very fortuitous. Ulanda is a gifted attorney. I predict that she will be tapped for a senior government position one day. When I went to Mexico City on a fact finding trip, I discovered that Nineball Express had committed a number of illegal actions that were well documented. I also discovered that Omnium Limited worked on Nineball's behalf. Apparently, there was some big time graft involved and Omnium had come in too late. As part of the damage control, I had the opportunity of meeting the Duke, himself.

Syd cut right to the point. He would do a favor for me if I would agree to the compromise that Syd had worked out that let Mexican truckers come over the border up to 100 miles. This would take care of border towns but would eliminate any full scale eroding of Nineball's rather lucrative market. It was a no-brainer for me. Of course I agreed. This all came to pass around the end of June.

Now Syd was in my pocket. I wanted access to his services and in particular, the case at hand, damage control with Peter Simon and the whole Moses thing. The Duke proved worthy of his title. He tapped on grand jury sources that revealed that Joshua Kaplan, the Executive Director of Common Action, was working hard to insinuate that Peter Simon was guilty of murdering Moses Levi. Joshua's testimony (that occurred over four separate days) first prompted an FBI interrogation of Peter and then almost brought forth a murder indictment.

One can only speculate, but I think that Kaplan did this because he wanted to quash anyone's claim to the Humanity Hospitals case and to Fair Opportunity Initiative. Kaplan was set to be an empire builder. And this pair of cases proved very profitable from a donations point of view. Unfortunately, he could not live with Moses nor his successor, Peter Simon.

Kaplan banked on Moses folding when he cut all his funding in March. When I anted up to let it continue, this was an entirely unseen event. Kaplan had done his best to make Moses a pariah among all the usual suspects in town (for continued funding). What Joshua didn't know was the existence of Peter Simon.

Peter made all the difference. Once this became clear, Peter supplanted Moses as enemy number one. Now Joshua had two foes who might deny him the chance to make a very lucrative public policy issue his own: Moses and Peter. When Moses disappeared, there was only Peter left. Joshua tried his damnedest to get rid of Peter, too.

That was Joshua's big mistake—at least according to the FBI and the District Prosecutor. When I brought forth the handwritten journal, there was little doubt that Moses did not view Peter as an enemy. To the contrary, Peter had come around and had saved his cause. It was Josh Kaplan who was the antagonist. Therefore, it was Josh Kaplan who was charged in the murder of Moses Levi.

It was not the sort of career move that Josh had envisioned. The Board of Directors for Common Action suspended him immediately. And even after he was released due to a pre-trial motion concerning the equal possibility of the internet hate mail that Moses had received, no one was convinced. Joshua Kaplan was terminated as Director. I think he's now trying to establish some sort of social action law firm in the Midwest. Unless he's undergone a character transplant, I don't suspect that he'll succeed.

Josh had acted with a mission to rid himself of Moses Levi and supplant Moses as the leader of the cause. All of this is perfectly clear. It is also perfectly clear that Moses had many enemies—some of whom dated back to the Waste Disposal Systems, Inc. case. There were many who had a motive to kill Moses Levi.

So far there have been no other suspects brought to the bench.

I gave Ulanda free reign to settle the Humanity Hospitals Case just as she liked. She appreciated my intervention in the Mexican Trucking Consortium case so much that she has now agreed to become a senior partner in our law firm: Cohen, Potts, Sani, & Washington. She will bring in so much business, we'll have to open a new branch just for her.

And so it is that we move forward. The waves of the high tide coming in lap upon the pebbled shore. I hope that this swell, that has come upon me so suddenly, will carry me far onto the beach. But who knows if it will? Or where the next wave will come from?

THE JOURNAL OF MOSES LEVI: JUNE 25, 2000

My work with Common Action gave my life a certain direction for a time until Josh Kaplan made it rot from the inside. I am happy that I am rid of him and the organization he has perverted. But I can never be completely rid of him. They continue to prey on me. I honestly do not think they will be happy until I drop out of sight.

But my cause with the Fair Opportunity Initiative (including the Humanity Hospitals Case) has sustained me after I left the regular workforce. Since my change in life, I have often seen hope. The various battles have helped me live. Along with Miriam, they are what I live for. But sometimes I feel that the Cause is greater than all of us. Is the Cause G-d? Maimonides used to say that anything that is off the charts in perfection must be G-d. Was he correct?

Where will the Cause take me? Do I have any choice? I must continue to move Peter and his business clients over to our campaign. He is very reluctant. Perhaps it is wrong of me (given our history together), but I must work for the Good. Equal Opportunity for All advances us toward the Good. What could be a greater Cause?

THE JOURNAL OF MOSES LEVI:
JUNE 26, 2000

Peter came to a meeting with Saul and myself. Peter was emotionally detached. He does not understand the deadlines I'm working under.

THE JOURNAL OF MOSES LEVI:
JUNE 30, 2000—2 P.M.

I was talking to Josh today (he called me) about the upcoming vote in the Senate. It is rather dicey. If the votes aren't there, then they won't do anything. The majority and minority whips are getting a firm count today.

I couldn't help but feel that something was up with him. Perhaps he is more cunning than I ever realized. Perhaps he's really evil.

Today is my last day on this case unless I can get Cohen, Potts, and Sani to renew their support of me. I thought we had an agreement in Congress, but things are beginning to unravel.

I feel impotent. Can I get us there? I don't know. If the votes aren't there, then it won't happen. This is important.

THE JOURNAL OF MOSES LEVI:
JUNE 30, 2000—10 P.M.

Saul called. Cohen, Potts, and Sani have come through! They will back me for another 60 days. Peter has come through for me after all.

THE JOURNAL OF MOSES LEVI:
JULY 3, 2000

The votes in the Senate weren't there. The end's in sight. If they will only pass the bill! So close. So close. Will I be able to get there? Or will that be denied to me? What is most important, is helping the people. Fair opportunity for all people. If this can be achieved, who cares who is the leader?

Other Novels by Michael Boylan

Rainbow Curve, (2014) Fans of baseball's history will appreciate this compelling tale about race, politics, and corrupting power and one man's courage to stand up against it. *De Anima* #1

The Extinction of Desire (2007) What would you do if you suddenly became rich?. *De Anima* #2

Maya (Forthcoming) Follow the fate of an Irish-American family through three generations. It's the story of immigrants. *De Anima* #4.

Naked Reverse (2016) There is a backdoor to the ivory tower. Find out what happens to one professor who escapes. *Arche* #1

Georgia (Forthcoming) A novel told in three parts. Explore racial identity through a murder mystery set in the early 20th century. *Arche* #2-4

www.ingramcontent.com/pod-product-compliance
Lightning Source LLC
Chambersburg PA
CBHW060402030726
47497CB00003B/816